Dr Russell was laughing to himself.

'I just gave you an extremely provocative conversational opening, and you murmured a polite nothing.'

'Oh, I'm sorry, did you want to discuss it?'

Tom was still laughing. 'Actually, I thought I didn't. I thought I'd be relieved that you didn't pick my comment apart and use it for deep amateur psychoanalysis. But then, when you didn't say anything at all, I found I was disappointed.'

'So you've learnt something, haven't you?' Belinda retorted. 'That you're thoroughly contrary!'

Dear Reader

RAW DEAL is second in Caroline Anderson's trilogy, in which Maggie is manipulated by her grandmother into discovering appearances can deceive. We go to Australia for Lilian Darcy's A PRIVATE ARRANGEMENT, where Belinda Jones cares for a pregnant diabetic—problems! Clare Mackay unfolds SISTER PENNY'S SECRET, in her second novel, and Elizabeth Petty returns with THE SURGEON FROM FRANCE, where a delightful old patient plays matchmaker. Have fun!

The Editor

Lilian Darcy is Australian, but on her marriage made her home in America. She writes for theatre, film and television, as well as romantic fiction, and she likes winter sports, music, travel and the study of languages. Hospital volunteer work and friends in the medical profession provide the research background for her novels; she enjoys being able to create realistic modern stories, believable characters, and a romance that will stand the test of time.

Recent titles by the same author:

THE BECKHILL TRADITION
CLOSER TO A STRANGER

A PRIVATE ARRANGEMENT

BY

LILIAN DARCY

MILLS & BOON LIMITED
ETON HOUSE   18–24 PARADISE ROAD
RICHMOND   SURREY   TW9 1SR

*First published in Great Britain 1993
by Mills & Boon Limited*

© Lilian Darcy 1993

*Australian copyright 1993
Philippine copyright 1993
This edition 1993*

ISBN 0 263 77981 5

*Set in 10 on 11½ pt Linotron Times
03-9301-55878*

*Typeset in Great Britain by Centracet, Cambridge
Made and printed in Great Britain*

CHAPTER ONE

'YOU'VE got a crush on him, haven't you?' Deana Davenport said slyly, jabbing Belinda Jones with a sharp elbow as they both watched the retreating form of a certain endocrine specialist.

'Of course I haven't,' answered Belinda, too quickly and much too warmly.

She bit her lip and turned away from the older nurse. After over a year on the specialised endocrine ward here at Coronation Hospital, she was well aware of Deana's deserved reputation as a malicious gossip, and knew that her heated denial would only pique the older girl's interest.

With chestnut-brown hair and classical bone-structure but rather coarse skin, Sister Davenport could have been quite pretty if her face weren't permanently set in a narrow repertoire of sly looks and cruel smiles. Rumour had it that an unhappy love-affair was at the root of her unpleasant nature. Another rumour countered that she had *always* been unpleasant and had thus never *had* a love-affair, unhappy or otherwise.

Whatever the case, the story of Sister Jones's ridiculous crush on Dr Tom Russell would be all over the hospital by the end of the day, and Belinda, feeling like a helpless little fish struggling in a vast invisible net, didn't know what to do about it.

She *did* have a crush on Dr Russell, of course. An awful one. And while other girls in a similar position might dream of actually being in his arms one day, Belinda was far too level-headed to fool herself in such a way. She was twenty-two, and unusually innocent and inexperienced for her age—lacking not just sexual experience, but experience of the wider world in general. She was an ordinary nurse. She wasn't rich, she wasn't brilliant, and she wasn't even particularly pretty, she considered, with her fine, not-quite-blonde hair, her small features and petite build.

Dr Russell, on the other hand, was a very successful man in his mid-thirties, an endocrine specialist with a growing reputation, and he moved in some of the highest spheres of Brisbane society. Belinda knew this because she had seen his photograph in the social pages of the newspaper more than once. She had been tempted to cut out the photographs and keep them, but she hadn't.

And to top it all off, he was gorgeous. Or Belinda thought so, anyway. With dark hair cut quite short so that it revealed his classically shaped head, a deep tan finished with some light freckles, piercing blue eyes and a mouth that was generous in laughter and very straight and sober when he was absorbed in work, he had become the standard against which any other man she met was measured. . .and fell short.

She had been amazed to find that he wasn't married, and waited painfully for the announcement of an engagement, or a sizzling scandalous affair. Whatever the case, Belinda knew, in her quietly realistic way, that he was light years beyond her world, and barely aware of her existence, so she simply kept her head down whenever he was on the ward, said very little, and suffered.

'Look, he's coming back!' whispered Deana Davenport, her consonants hissing in her eagerness. 'And you're blushing! God, you're unreal!'

If Belinda had been a more devious soul, she might

have thought to suggest that Deana's harping on the subject of Dr Russell spoke rather strongly of a crush on *her* side as well, but Belinda *wasn't* devious, so she simply blushed even more and found on the desk in front of her a diabetic patient's chart that suddenly needed her urgent attention. She had been feeling like this about Dr Russell for nearly a year. Surely it would have to go away soon? If only he *would* announce his engagement! Perhaps that would make this weakness in her knees, whenever she saw him, disappear.

Her heart thudded painfully as he leaned over the high beige bench top that bordered this part of the nurses' station and spoke absently to Deana. 'Er— Sister, I need Sharon Blackett's case-file.'

'I'm sure *Belinda* can help you with that,' the other nurse replied archly.

'Belinda!' he frowned impatiently. 'Who——? Oh, yes—Sister Jones. Thanks.'

Belinda had the case-file in front her and had handed it over without a word almost before he had realised who she was. He crossed the corridor in two strides and sat in a small room that was used for counselling or small case conferences, leaving the door open and flipping impatiently through the file.

Deana watched both him and Belinda out of the corner of her eye. The latter, riffling some more paperwork furiously and uselessly, wondered to herself if this was the reason Deana squinted so horribly—she spent so much time trying to spy on two people at once. Then she felt ashamed of the malicious thought, and realised that that was one of the most dangerous things about people like Deana. They gave everyone around them a more unpleasant outlook on life.

'You haven't got a hope, you know,' Deana whispered suddenly. 'If you're staying on this ward because you think he'll notice you and start asking you out—him or any other good-looking doctor—then you'll be here till Doomsday.'

"Well, you're wrong there, anyway,' Belinda retorted forcefully, taking herself by surprise as well as Deana. 'I certainly won't be here till Doomsday, or even till Christmas. As it happens, I'm planning to leave soon to. . .to do some private nursing for a year or two before going overseas.'

'Really? That's the first I've heard of it,' said Deana, narrowing her muddy brown eyes suspiciously.

That she hadn't heard of the plan was scarcely surprising, since Belinda had made it up on the spur of the moment. She was just thinking dizzily that perhaps it was what she really *should* do, in order to get Dr Russell out of her system, when Sharon Blackett's fat file was dumped unceremoniously on top of the rest of the paperwork and she looked up to see the endocrinologist's painfully disturbing form looming over her. She stood up instinctively, but he still seemed to tower above her. He must be at least six feet two, she decided confusedly, wondering why those blue eyes turned her legs to jelly so quickly.

'Sister—er—Jones?'

'Yes?'

'This is none of my business, but did I just hear you say you were thinking of doing some private nursing to save for an overseas trip?'

'Yes, you did,' Belinda answered, stepping back a pace. The chair behind her knees scraped on the floor with a raucous metallic sound, and she winced. With Deana still listening, she could scarcely claim that he had misheard.

'Because it's likely that I have a job for you, if you're

interested. I know of someone who needs a nurse who's experienced in diabetic patient care.'

Belinda heard Deana's hissing intake of breath, and for a moment she was tempted to lay a hand on Dr Russell's arm in an intimate gesture and say, 'It sounds perfect, Doctor! Why don't we meet for a drink this evening to discuss it?'

But she knew that any attempt at this sort of seductive sophistication would be laughably incongruous coming from her quiet, ordinary little self, and in any case she had made no serious plans to leave, so she simply said steadily, 'That's very nice of you, Dr Russell, but I haven't fully worked out my plans yet, and if I do leave I'll probably sign on with a nursing agency. I'm sure your friend will have no trouble finding someone.'

'OK,' he shrugged easily. 'Just a thought. Let me know if you change your mind over the next week or so.'

'Of course. Thank you, Doctor,' she murmured. But he was already on his way out of the ward.

'"Of course. Thank you, Doctor",' Deana mimicked with an exaggerated simper, as soon as Tom Russell was safely out of earshot. 'Why did you turn it down?'

'Oh, because I. . .' Stupid! She had hesitated again. I'm just putty in the hands of someone like Deana, she decided, angry at herself.

"Because you don't have any plans to leave at all!' jeered Deana. 'You just said that so I'd stop teasing you about Tom Russell.' Her tone caressed the name briefly. 'Which just *proves* you're infatuated with him. Cheer up! If you can't get him, there's always Dr Entwistle. You might have a chance with him!'

Laughing at this last jibe, she swept some papers into her arms and went over to the far side of the nurses' station, where files were stored, leaving Belinda relieved to be alone. That last comment had particularly sickened her. Stephen Entwistle was not one of the younger, more dynamic doctors. In his mid-forties, he was a quiet man and a noted specialist in thyroid problems, but not even his best friend could call him handsome. It was typical of Deana that she thought Belinda 'might have a chance' with the man just because he was ugly.

In fact, he was married, although not many people knew this, and his wife had a serious and incurable disease called lupus, which at times took quite a toll on his own emotions and energy. Belinda had stumbled upon him one day several months ago when he was alone in a little-used store-room at the far end of the ward, and she had seen immediately that he was near to breaking down. After a heart-to-heart talk, she had gently ordered him home for the rest of the week, and since that time they had been friends in a reserved sort of way. The fact that he obviously thought she was a good nurse pleased her and gave her confidence, while the fact that Belinda had not betrayed his secret and gossiped about his wife and her illness earned his gratitude and respect, so that now they were allies and she knew she would be able to go to him if ever she had a problem at the hospital.

Was Deana Davenport a problem in that sense? No, she decided after a short reflection. Gossip and teasing were things you had to deal with by yourself, and the best way to deal with them was to forget about them. Accordingly, she quietly left the nurses' station to go and take her patients' before-lunch blood sugars, and carefully avoided Deana for the rest of the shift. She could not avoid her in the nurses' home dining-room that night, however.

The older nurse came up to her as she put salad, chicken with vegetables and a cup of tea on to her tray in the cafeteria-style serving area. 'Did you see Tom Russell in the car park this afternoon?' she asked.

'No, I didn't,' Belinda answered evenly.

'Did *you* see him, Sarah?' Deana said to the girl just ahead of Belinda, who was, unfortunately, another of the less pleasant nurses.

'No, why? What was he doing?' plump-cheeked Sarah asked through a mouthful of the bread roll she was chomping on.

'Who was he *with* you mean!' Deana crowed triumphantly. 'This gorgeous redhead, obviously stinking rich. She was piled with jewellery. But poor little Belinda here thinks he's going to fall in love with *her*!'

'Oh, crikey!' sighed Sarah. 'If I had a dollar for every nurse in this hospital who's been infatuated with Tom Russell over the past four years, *I'd* be stinking rich too!'

'There!' Deana turned to Belinda. 'Will that convince you you're wasting your time?'

'The only way I'm wasting my time is by talking to *you*!' Belinda retorted, her voice high and tight.

She had done nothing to deserve Deana's petty jibes, and suddenly it was too much. The picture of the gorgeous redhead was very vivid in her mind as well, and she knew that there Deana spoke the truth. Her helpless feelings for Dr Russell *were* a waste of time. Unfortunately that didn't make them go away.

Picking up her tray without the fruit and cake she had planned to take, Belinda left the cafeteria line with tight lips and stiffened shoulders, but, before she had gone very far, Deana had caught up to her, grabbing her upper arm roughly and painfully so that her hot dinner spilled on to the tray and splashed her wrist.

'You just think you're so wonderful, don't you? No one here likes you, the way you sit off by yourself at meals half the time as if you're waiting for someone who's good enough for you. You think I'm a bitch, don't you? Well, I'm only doing it for your own good. It's about time someone hit you with a dose of reality!'

With this, she released Belinda abruptly, and the chicken dinner went slopping over on to the tray again. Belinda put it down on the nearest table and sat there, shaking and desperately trying not to show how upset she was over Deana's blunt accusation. Was it true? No one liked her? Everyone thought she was stuck up? Had her shyly determined efforts to be friendly with the other quieter girls like herself been so thoroughly misinterpreted? She tried to look at the thing calmly and sensibly, tried not to be aware of Deana and Sarah whispering at a table only a few yards distant, but felt too hurt and shocked to be rational.

Someone with more experience of the rough and tumble of friendships, jealousies and animosities might have been able to dismiss Deana's words as the unmotivated expressions of bitterness and jealousy that they were, but Belinda was inexperienced, and although she knew enough about Deana to be wary and distrustful she did not know enough to ignore her as fully as she should.

After picking at her meal, she fled to her room and hid there, venturing out only once in search of a friendly nurse from the postnatal ward, Louise Hickson, with whom she hoped to talk the matter through. But there was no answer when she knocked on Louise's door, nor when she tried another new friend's door at the far end of the passage, and this was so discouraging that she went back to her own room and cried till her blue eyes wre red-rimmed and swollen.

The next day she had the whole thing in perspective again, especially after she did find Louise at lunch and told her as much of the story as she could without mentioning Tom Russell. But Deana's persecution, continued more subtly and covertly as the days went by, had left its sting, and she began to wonder if living in the nurses' home was really the right thing. Perhaps she shouldn't have dismissed Dr Russell's offer of private nursing work so quickly.

'Listen, Sister Jones.'

Belinda's head flew up to meet the blue onslaught of Tom Russell's frowning gaze. She hadn't heard his approach, having been absorbed in struggling with an unusually detailed report on the condition of a pregnant diabetic and her unborn twins—one of Dr Russell's patients, actually.

'Yes, Doctor?'

'Can I see you for a minute?'

'Of course. I——'

'Finish that later,' he commanded, dismissing her paperwork.

She rose obediently and followed him into the small counselling-room across the corridor from the nurses' station, relieved to remember that Deana Davenport had the day off today. The other nurse would get weeks of mileage out of Belinda incurring a reprimand from Dr Russell, if that was what this was.

Could it be that? she wondered, in the few seconds before he spoke. Running her mind quickly over the events of the week just passed, she couldn't think of anything she had done wrong, and Tom Russell was not the kind of doctor who made mountains out of molehills where nursing procedure was concerned. She had seen more of him over the past few days than she usually did, however, so perhaps there *was* something. . .

'I wanted to ask you again about this private nursing job.'

She looked at him mutely, wishing very fervently that she had never invented the stupid lie for Deana's benefit. Dr Russell was taking her seriously, and she was wasting his time. Or was she? The idea of doing some private nursing, then perhaps travelling for a while, had stayed in the back of her mind during the days since that disastrous exchange with Deana in the cafeteria, and a small voice kept saying inside her, 'Perhaps you should. Now, with Dr Russell himself taking the idea so seriously. . .

'Is anything wrong?' he queried, and Belinda realised that she had been staring at him in silence for far too long, as she tried to decide what to say.

'No,' she answered quickly, 'nothing at all.' Then, taking a deep breath as if she were about to plunge into a pool of unknown depth and temperature— which, perhaps, she was—she continued, 'But could you tell me a bit more about what the work would entail?'

She saw his brow clear. 'Of course,' he said, in that deep, rich tone that sent funny tingles up her spine. 'Stupid of me! Here I am wondering whether you'd be suitable, and whether Faye will like you, and you don't even know what's involved. For a start, it's a live-in position. Does that bother you?'

'That depends. . .'

'On the house,' he finished for her, although it hadn't been what she was thinking. 'Don't worry—it's a huge, beautiful place, quite centrally located, and you'll have your own room. Suite, actually, you could call it.'

'A suite?' That sounded intriguingly glamorous

'Yes—bedroom, bathroom, a door opening on to a section of enclosed veranda, and an open veranda beyond that, looking down on to a rather beautiful tropical garden. But we're getting out of order.'

'Yes, we are,' she murmured, hating her reaction to their close proximity.

His knees jutted just out of reach in the low black vinyl chair opposite her, and somehow this made her tongue feel like cotton wool. She tried looking out of the window to the hospital's green lawns and the tall eucalypts that stood motionless against a gloriously blue August sky, but found that looking away seemed too impolite.

'I'll be brief,' he went on, as she turned back to him. 'My sister Faye is a Type One diabetic—onset at age fifteen, with some past incidence of proliferative retinopathy that now seems under control, fortunately. She's thirty-eight now, and pregnant, very keen to have a baby, but *highly* at risk for a number of reasons, as you may imagine. But she refuses to spend the next seven months in hospital—and I can't say I blame her. A long hospital stay like that would be demoralising to anyone.' And his tone clearly implied that his sister wasn't just 'anyone'. 'So she needs fairly constant care at home. I've been staying at her place for some weeks now, in order to help her maintain the tight control on her blood sugar that's so vital, especially in the first three months, but that's becoming impractical. I need to focus on my work here, and my sister and I are beginning to drive each other mad.'

' Oh dear. . .' Belinda drawled gently, having some understanding of sibling irritations herself.

He grimaced. 'Actually, I packed my bags last night and went home. Faye's going to be a difficult patient, frankly, and she's fussy about who she'll have——' He broke off and smiled suddenly, his mouth wryly crooked and some small, fine wrinkles forming at the corners of his fathomless blue eyes. 'I'm not making this sound very attractive, am I?'

'Well, the house sounds lovely,' Belinda blurted, then flushed as he threw back his head and laughed, his long tanned throat exposed to her tremulous gaze.

'But my sister sounds like a witch,' he finished for her, evidently extremely amused by the idea. 'She's not, actually. She's very nice. But she's a woman of decided opinions.'

'Then won't she want to see me before she agrees to take me on?'

'Then you *do* want the job!'

Belinda could have kicked herself. A part of her— the silly, hopeless part—*did* want the job, of course, because it meant that she would see Dr Russell, since it was his own sister she would be nursing. The sensible part, however, knew that seeing him would only be painful and that if she was to get over this miserable crush she ought to do everything possible to stay away from the man.

Unfortunately, seeing the keen glint in his eye and the impatient energy to get the thing settled that he was betraying, she didn't quite know how to turn him down.

'I. . . I——' she stammered.

'Don't worry—Faye trusts my judgement. . .in this area, anyway. If I say you're good, she'll have you. But she's already rejected four agency nurses now, so I'm getting a bit desperate.'

'But what makes you so sure I *am* good?' Belinda tried desperately.

'I've been watching you over the past few days.' He had too, she realised, although she had been too absorbed in her own clumsy, hopeless awareness of him to have taken the fact in until now. 'Steve

Entwistle speaks very highly of you as well, and he's a man whose opinion I respect a lot. He said that as well as your meticulous attention to detail—so important with diabetic care—you had an infallible instinct for when a person was in pain. Emotional pain, he meant, not physical.'

'He said that?'

'Yes.' He studied her curiously and then spoke in a slow, thoughtful way. 'And he didn't know what had given it to you. . .'

It was clearly intended as a question about her personal life, and, after a short hesitation, she decided that he had the right to an answer, if she really was going to take the job—and she now suspected gloomily that she was. It was Dr Entwistle who had prodded her more firmly in that direction, oddly enough. If he felt that she had something genuine to give, then perhaps she should go ahead and give it.

'My mother died when I was ten,' she answered Tom Russell carefully. 'My father has only just fully recovered from his grief. Oh, he's always functioned perfectly well as a father and in his work. . .'

'What does he do?' he asked.

'Well, he was a farmer, out west near Emerald. Then when we moved to Brisbane he bought a hardware shop.'

'Do you have brothers and sisters?'

'Yes. Brothers—three. The older one is eighteen and the twins are fourteen.'

'And your father has. . .what? A full-time house-keeper?' he asked.

'No.'

'But he did when you were younger?'

'No. He. . .couldn't afford anyone,' Belinda explained.

'Then how did you manage?'

'We all did our share.'

'But you're the eldest, so. . .'

'Yes,' she acknowledged reluctantly, lifting her small chin so that her fine hair fell away from her face, 'I did quite a bit.'

He nodded and clearly recognised the answer for what it was—an understatement. Belinda had worked very hard indeed for nearly twelve years since her mother's death, becoming almost a mother herself to the twin boys and doing as much of the cooking and housekeeping as she could between school and homework. There had been almost no time for friends, let alone parties, outings or boyfriends.

But she did not resent the life she had led. Her father had worked just as hard, and the boys too, when they were old enough. Neither had her father been ungrateful. When he realised that none of his children was interested in farming as a career, he had moved the family to Brisbane and had encouraged Belinda in her ambition to become a nurse.

Then, three months ago, he had suggested that she had done enough for himself and the boys. The hardware shop was at last doing well now, the boys were growing up, and he could afford part-time housekeeping. 'Why don't you move into the nurses' home at the hospital, make some friends and have some fun?' he had suggested, and Belinda had done so.

At least, she had moved. The friends and fun part wasn't so easy. After those years of hard work, she didn't quite know how to be social and high-spirited and careless of the future like so many other girls of her own age. Some of her ideas about sex and marriage seemed old-fashioned compared with various loudly expressed opinions she had heard from other nurses, and her steps towards the lighter side of life were still very tentative, as Deana's blunt accusations last week had shown her. She was beginning to tackle the problem in her quietly determined way, by suggesting a movie or a shopping trip to one or two of the quieter girls in the nurses' home, and by spending more time chatting with her patients instead of being simply a sympathetic presence.

But Tom Russell wouldn't want to know any of this. In fact—— She started a little as he muttered a gruff exclamation. He was looking at his watch. 'Lord, is that the time? I didn't intend this to take more than a minute. I have to run.' He was on his feet at once, seeming to fill the room with that energetic figure. 'Faye needs someone as soon as possible now, so perhaps I'd better square it with the hospital for you. And of course you'll want to meet each other before the thing is finalised. What time does your shift finish today?'

'Three'

'Hmm. I can't get away until four. Can you wait for me in the foyer of the nurses' home at ten past and we'll run over to Faye and Bill's in my car?'

'But. . .' The word came out like a helpless little bleat as Belinda followed him out of the room.

'What's the problem?' He turned, irritated and frowning, and the instinctive objection died on her lips.

'Did you say ten past four?' she said weakly, and after a quick nod he was striding down the corridor, to disappear through the swing door that marked the boundary of the endocrine ward's domain.

CHAPTER TWO

'WELL, you're all dressed up to the nines!'

Belinda flinched as she saw who it was that had come out of the lift and addressed her. Deana Davenport, of course, and her catty comment had been somewhat inaccurate. Belinda wasn't really dressed up to the nines. Deana, rather, was dressed *down* in old jeans and a slightly stained white blouse, finished off with worn thongs. She had evidently only come down to the foyer to collect her mail.

'Waiting for your boyfriend?' the older nurse suggested sarcastically.

'Yes, he's picking me up any minute,' Belinda answered Deana in a moment of daring wickedness. 'We're going down to Redland Bay to have dinner on his boat and go for a sail,' she invented fluently.

It was only just four o'clock now, so Dr Russell should stay safely out of the way for another ten minutes, by which time Deana would be gone again.

'Sailing? Dressed like that?' Deana returned, clearly sceptical.

Belinda immediately perceived the flaws in her story. A gilt clip fastened her fine hair in a high ponytail, and this peach-toned dress of Sea Island cotton, although it was fairly plain with its simply cut bodice, high-neck, elbow sleeves and knee-length pleated skirt, wasn't what any sensible person would wear sailing. She embroidered her tale quickly. 'Oh, I don't suppose us girls will do any actual crewing. We'll just sit around watching the men. My boyfriend likes me to dress well.'

'You've never mentioned your boyfriend before,' Deana observed.

Belinda shifted her sandalled feet nervously, wondering suddenly if Deana had decided to hang around until the mythical sailor showed up. The minutes were creeping by. 'Oh, we prefer to keep our relationship very private at this stage,' she answered the other nurse, sounding much less assured, now, to her own ears, and regretting that she had started this silly game. Paying Deana Davenport back in her own coin always seemed to backfire.

'Really? You can tell me his first name, though, can't you? That won't give anything away,' cajoled Deana, and it was at that moment that an open-topped, low-slung dark red sports car purred to an impatient halt directly in front of the foyer's big glass doors and the unmistakable silhouette of Tom Russell sprang with athletic grace from behind the wheel and began to stride across the cement footpath towards the entrance.

'Oh, there's Dr Russell! My goodness, I think he wants to speak to me!' Belinda improvised at a gabble through a strained throat, and she hurried through the doors before Dr Russell could reach them and before Deana Davenport could gather her wits enough to reply.

Ensconced in his car a moment later—and goodness, it felt luxurious!—she glanced back at the foyer and saw that the other girl stood there staring with narrowed, suspicious eyes. Her heart sank. Deana would not easily forgive Belinda's silly attempt to trick her, and she had the power to make life miserable for some time to come. Then something else struck her. Heaven help her if the other girl really did think she was involved with Dr Russell!

'I managed to get away a touch early,' the endocrine specialist said as the car slid out of the parking bay and into the main driveway, then wound through the open, grassy grounds to join an arterial road that ran along the winding Brisbane River. 'Thanks for being so punctual. You saved me a trip up to your room to collect you.'

'Oh, I'm always early for things,' Belinda confessed naïvely. As soon as they were out of the grounds, petty concerns about Deana Davenport and hospital gossip washed cleanly away, made surprisingly unimportant by the relaxing hum of Tom Russell's car as they drove. She went on, 'Mother used to say it was so rude to keep people waiting, because it implied that you thought your time was more precious than theirs.' She wasn't aware of how her voice softened when she said the word 'Mother', although she did know that the precepts of morality and etiquette that she remembered her mother spelling out to her were the ones she kept most assiduously.

Tom Russell was silent for a minute, after one brief glance at her, then he gave a cheerful bark of laughter. 'I like that reasoning,' he said. 'The only trouble is, my sister Faye *does* think her time is more precious than other people's. She's bound to be fussing with something or other when we arrive, and we'll be twiddling our thumbs for twenty minutes before she condescends to appear.'

'Oh, I'm sorry, I didn't meant to imply. . .to insult——' Belinda began, but he silenced her with a pat on the knee that made her tingle frighteningly all over.

'Hey!' he laughed. 'I'm criticising Faye, not you. Don't be a mouse. You don't need to be.'

And after that rather cryptic last sentence, he was silent, which meant that Belinda chose to be so as well. Actually, she was rather glad that she didn't have to talk. . .or listen to that deep voice which she found so compelling and disturbing. If they had been chatting, no matter how lightly, she would have been so absorbed in carefully listening and in getting out a reply through a nervously constricted throat that she wouldn't have been able to enjoy this wonderful drive.

Needless to say, she had never been in a sports car before, and to be speeding and curving through the streets with the top open and the balmy August breeze combing silkily through her fine hair was sheer heaven. Queensland's short, mild winter was slipping easily into a vibrant spring, and tropical plants and shrubs were beginning to fill the gardens they passed with a colourful bounty of flowers.

Belinda didn't know exactly where they were going, and in her five hard-working years in Brisbane had never been through these opulent suburbs before, but in a way it was nicer to surrender herself to a mystery drive. With Tom Russell at the wheel she instinctively knew that nothing could go wrong. He drove so smoothly and the tyres hummed so pleasantly on the tarred road that she knew she could easily have slept. The leather bucket seat held her slender figure in a cushioned caress, and trees overhanging the road softened the strong Queensland sunlight with patches of blurred green shade.

On each side of the road she caught glimpses of distinctive Queensland-style houses, these ones all large, carefully restored and lovingly maintained. Belinda's father had of necessity bought a rather characterless cream brick house in the outer suburb where his hardware shop was located, and Belinda had always wanted to live in one of these gracious old places, which were larger, more urban versions of the old farmhouse near Emerald where she had spent her childhood.

The raised, open dwellings made sense in this tropical climate. The stilt-like wooden pillars lifted the single-storeyed living space anything up to twelve feet off the ground, and the open space underneath, which allowed breezes to flow beneath the house to keep it cool, was usually enclosed with light wooden laticework. Wide wooden verandas often surrounded a house on all four sides, although sometimes a part of the veranda had been enclosed to provide extra living space.

'What's the name of this suburb?' she asked impulsively.

'Indooroopilly.' The melodic Aboriginal word flowed smoothly on his tongue, pronounced more like 'Indra-pilly' in spite of all those oos.

'Indooroopilly,' she repeated, enjoying the name. 'And is this where your sister, Mrs—er. . . .'

'Hamilton,' he supplied for her.

'Hamilton. Is this where she lives?'

'Yes. And I do too, as it happens, although my place is smaller and further from the river. We're almost there.' He made a turn as he spoke, then said, 'This is my sister's street.'

The delicious ride had to end, of course, but as Tom Russell turned into a driveway paved with red herring-bone-patterned brick, Belinda felt she was surrendering a very precious experience. Was it the open-topped car? The perfect day? The lushly leafed suburbs? Or just the company of the man behind the wheel. She had a horrible suspicion that it was far too much of the latter.

It was a timely realisation, and cured her instantly of the lingering dream state the drive had produced in her. She had been tired after her early shift, which had necessitated getting up at six; perhaps that was why she had slipped so easily into that state of contented, almost hypnotic languor.

Squaring her shoulders and remembering that what lay ahead was, after all, a job interview, she followed Dr Russell up the long flight of steps at the front of the house and through a wooden latticework door on to a cool veranda where outdoor furniture splashed with warm tropical colours was invitingly arranged.

'Sit down,' the endocrinologist suggested, 'and I'll go and look for Faye.'

Before he could do so, however, an aproned, curly-haired housekeeper appeared through a side door, pushing it open with one of her ample hips as both hands were occupied in bearing a tray. On it, tall glasses rattled lightly against a green glass jug that clinked with ice, floating on top of a cool blend of tropical fruit juices.

'Mrs Hamilton wants you to sit down,' Mrs Porter said after Dr Russell had made brief introductions. 'She says she'll only be a few minutes.'

'Does she, now?' Tom murmured mildly, and a bubble of laughter rose to Belinda's lips.

She suppressed it quickly and guiltily, but not before she had been rewarded by an equally amused glance from Dr Russell, which had the unfortunate effect of turning all her limbs to jelly at once. Hastily she sat down, and was relieved when the tall doctor took a seat safely distant from her own and reached to the table that separated them to pour her a long drink of the invitingly iced fruit juice. Her throat felt parched all of a sudden.

They sipped their drinks in silence for several minutes while Belinda took in the details of house and garden. The place was painted in a cool, glossy white with forest-green trim, and the thick, shiny foliage of tropical trees and shrubs pressed closely against the house at several points to create pools of dappled shade.

Below her on the lawn she could see the sculpted form of a stone fountain with water spilling from its lips into a fish- and lily-filled pond. In summer, that gushing sound would be refreshingly cool and delightfully soporific. In fact the whole place seemed geared towards just what she and Dr Russell were doing now—sipping cool drinks and dreaming the afternoon away.

She was roused from this reverie seconds later when he gulped the last of the juice and said, 'I know what Faye's "few minutes" mean. Finish your drink and let's go inside. I'll give you a tour of the house and show you your room. . . That is, if you take the job,' he added as an afterthought, frowning.

Belinda gulped her juice and followed him obediently, too aware of him as he stood back to make way for her, or strode ahead to open a door, the taut muscles in arms and thighs revealed by his economical movements.

She soon decided that the house was the most beautiful place she had ever seen, and though she had little experience of antique furniture or fine art works she immediately recognised that all the things she saw were of the highest quality. Dark hardwood floors, polished to a deep, waxy glass, and plain white walls provided a simple backdrop for throw-rugs, tapestries, ornate cabinets and large pottery urns or figurines standing on carved stands. Everything had an Oriental feel to it, which was just right for this cool, tropical house, and the large rooms were not crowded with pieces but gave a feeling of tranquil, uncluttered space. Belinda thrilled at once to the beauty of it all, and knew that she would enjoy the opportunity of finding out more about where all these lovely things came from . . .if she took the job, she reminded herself hastily, just as Dr Russell had recently done, even while she suspected that the matter was a foregone conclusion.

He led the way through a large and ultra-modern kitchen, with glass-fronted cabinets in pale natural wood and what seemed like acres of bench space in white marble swirled with pale grey, surrounding a glass stove-top and double sink. Behind the glass cabinet doors, Belinda glimpsed rows of neatly labelled spice jars and piles of elegant crockery—all the pride and delight of the housekeeper Mrs Porter, evidently— then they had passed through the kitchen and into an enclosed section of veranda where the hardwood floor gave way to squares of woven sea-grass matting.

'This is your space,' the endocrinologist said. 'Mrs Porter uses it or this small room off it, just here, as a sitting-room occasionally, but she doesn't live in, so you would virtually have the run of this part of the house.'

He opened a white-painted door with a stained glass transom window above it, then stood back so that Belinda could enter first. 'And this is your room,' he said.

She stood transfixed, and didn't notice the expression of intrigued interest that he wore as he watched her. After her small bedroom at home, where beloved old ornaments belonging once to her mother jostled for space with a basket of ironing she hadn't yet had time for, and nursing textbooks that wouldn't fit on her one small bookshelf, or her room at the nurses' home, where exotic travel posters—gleaned from a travel agent next to her father's hardware shop—couldn't disguise the institutional plainness of the furnishings, this room seemed palatial.

The expanse of wooden floor, cool and clean and shining. . .the double bed with its hand-appliquéd quilt in a complex pattern of pastels and white. . .the stand of leafy potted plants, the antique free-standing mirror, whose glass oval would take in the whole length of a woman in evening dress. . .the modern wardrobe, built-in, that blended so skilfully into the architectural mood of the house while providing all the space for clothing that she could possibly need. . .two original paintings on the walls, each an impressionistic landscape in subtle, imaginative colour. . . There was even a carved wooden rocking chair.

'You can take that out on to the veranda if you like,' Tom Russell told her as she reached out to touch its polished arm-rest.

He opened a second door, which again had an elegant stained glass transom above it, and Belinda found it led to an open veranda that must connect with the one they had sat on for drinks. She was about to go out to it, but he called her back, opening a third door in the rear wall of the room. 'And this is the bathroom.'

As she looked into it, she tried not to let slip just what a luxury this was. It was the first bathroom she had ever had to herself, and sharing with three younger brothers—she had found tadpoles in her toothglass once—had its share of perils. The cool, tiled expanse, done in simple blue and white, gleamed, and the brass fixtures glowed like well-worn gold.

'Will it do?' Dr Russell asked in a low, gently teasing voice, still studying her closely, with that smile that came and went around his lips.

She flushed. He had guessed that this place was a palace to her, and she wondered suddenly if she was a complete fool even to consider getting mixed up in his world, when it was so far removed from her own. She felt as fragile and foolish as a moth that beat itself against the hot glass of an electric bulb until it fell burned and spent, in its desperate doomed quest for the light.

For the first time she realised that Deana Davenport's jealous bitterness wasn't the real danger. It was Tom Russell himself. If he ever guessed that she carried this stupid, hopeless torch for him, he would . . .what? She didn't even know. Laugh about it? Tell his friends? Despise her? Or simply feel sorry for her in an absentminded sort of way? Of all the possibilities, this last one seemed the worst, somehow.

'It's lovely,' she answered him at last, in a brisk, matter-of-fact tone that concealed, she hoped, all that she was feeling.

'*Lovely*, is it?' he echoed, not fooled at all. 'Good.'

'But if I take the job,' she blurted, goaded by the idea that he found her lack of sophistication amusing, 'it won't be because I like the house. Far from it.'

He frowned. 'What the——? I'm not suggesting it would be.'

She heard the impatience in his tone and went on even more firmly, 'It would simply be that it fits in with my long-term plan, which is to get a wide range of experience before going on an extended working holiday overseas.'

'Well, of course,' he agreed. 'That sounds very sensible, if you want to travel. You don't have to justify your plans to me, or to anyone else.'

'No, I—I know.'

'Faye will be pleased, I think, if you do take the job,

because nurses experienced in pre-natal diabetic care are thin on the ground at nursing agencies these days. But it has to be your decision, Belinda.'

He had never used her first name before, she realised, and the lilting sound of it on his lips sent a knife-sharp thrust of awareness through her, taking away any power to reply to his last words. After a short silence in which they both stood there awkwardly, he said, impatient again, 'Faye *must* be ready by now! Let's go back.'

He took her the long way through the house again, and Belinda tried to orientate herself. He hadn't indicated where Faye's room was, and she wondered what would happen if she needed to monitor her patient during the night. Was there a bell?

Back on the veranda, the chairs were still empty, but before they could sit down there came the sound of footsteps and Faye Hamilton came around the corner of the house. She wore a loosely cut silk dress in vibrant tropical colours, mainly greens, which set off her wild halo of rusty-red hair, tanned skin and generous dappling of freckles. She had a wide, full mouth, a straight nose, and the same piercing blue eyes as her brother. You couldn't call Tom Russell's sister pretty, Belinda decided, but at the same time she knew that most men would be instantly attracted to Mrs Hamilton and would call her beautiful.

But there was more than beauty in her face today.

'I'm bleeding again, Tom,' his sister said without preamble. She had a hand pressed against the wall for support, and her hard tone and blunt words didn't fool Belinda into thinking she didn't care. There was heart-rending fear and hurt behind that energetic and vibrant façade.

'Faye! How much?'

'Oh, nothing dramatic—just the usual staining. But that's how it started both times before, and if I lose this baby, I'll——'

'Hey!' Tom was at his sister's side, not bothering with the niceties of introducing Belinda, to the latter's relief. 'Don't get into a state—that's not going to help. Lie down here on this lounge with——'

'My legs slightly raised and on my left side,' Faye finished for him, deliberately parroting the words. 'I've spent weeks of my life doing that in the past, and it hasn't helped.'

'But those miscarriages were ten and eleven years ago. You've stopped smoking and your blood sugar is consistently within the normal range since you started the self-care programme six years ago. There's every chance that this pregnancy will succeed. The ultrasound scan four weeks ago showed a normal "pregnancy ring" as they call it, which means there's a foetal sac in there, and——'

'Don't bully me with your logic and your jargon, Tom!' snapped Faye, reaching automatically for the brimming glass of sweet juice that stood on the small table beside her.

'I'm not bullying,' Tom retorted.

'Yes, you are. . . Oh!' She broke off, flexed her empty hand and looked in surprise at the cold-beaded glass Belinda had silently taken from her.

'I'm sorry,' Belinda said, 'but I wondered. . . Your blood sugar level. Naturally you're upset at the moment, and that kind of stress. . .'

'She's right, Faye,' Tom came in, after giving Belinda a long, frowning stare that made her words threaten to dry in her mouth.

His support of her unusual action came as a relief, and she willingly left the explanation to him. 'Stress can raise your blood sugar unexpectedly, and with that glass of sweet juice on top. . .'

Faye understood now too, and she sank back into the reclining lounge chair with a gesture of despair. 'I was taking my blood-sugar level when you arrived,' she said.

'And what was it?'

'A hundred and six.'

'That's fine,' he told her.

'But it was just after that that I discovered the bleeding, and I've been. . . I *am* upset. How can I keep within the normal range when this sort of thing happens? Yet keeping within the normal range is——'

'It *is* possible, Faye. You've been doing it, and it's *going* to continue!' Tom Russell spoke almost ferociously, and Belinda caught a glimpse, for the first time, of the love he had for his older sister, and the strong professional and personal commitment he had to this all-important pregnancy. He continued firmly, and Faye relaxed a little, as if half daring to believe him at last. '*That's* why you need hospitalisation. . .or a nurse. Someone to help you keep everything on an even keel for the whole pregnancy. . . So meet Belinda!'

'Yes. Belinda Jones,' the owner of the name said simply, and waited while Dr Russell's sister seemed to fully take in her presence for the first time.

'Hmm,' said Faye, after what seemed like several minutes. Her eyes were narrowed and her alert expression a contrast to her earlier tension. 'I thought all nurses had bad skin and beefy thighs.'

'Idiot!' Tom Russell exploded with friendly derision.

'Well, the four that agency sent me did. You, on the other hand. . .'

'Oh, I'm very strong,' Belinda put in helpfully. 'Much stronger than I look. I grew up on a farm.'

'I'm not concerned about your strength, love,' Faye Hamilton said, but she didn't bother to explain what she *was* concerned with. As she lay back with a plump cushion provided by her brother beneath her lower legs, she cocked her head to one side and studied Belinda, nodding in approval.

Then, with a teasing, apologetic smile at the young nurse, she said to her brother, 'She'll do, Tom. Thanks! When can she start?'

'Wait a minute, Faye. You've made up your mind in your usual uniquely wilful way, But Miss Jones may not have made up hers.'

'Oh, please call me Belinda,' blurted Miss Jones. 'Both of you.' She hated the more formal title.

'Well, Belinda? Do you——?' Faye prompted, but her brother interrupted once again.

'Give yourself some time, Nurse,' he said. 'Whisking you out here like this has probably put you under pressure to say yes, but please don't feel you have to take the job. It may not be right for you at all.'

He leaned forward as he spoke, his tanned forehead pleated into a concerned frown and his mouth set in a line of sober sincerity. Belinda felt bewildered by his apparent about-face. This morning, he wouldn't take no for an answer, and, after urging her to consider the idea and bringing her out here as confidently as if the whole thing were quite settled in his mind, he was now taking the ground from under her feet by playing devil's advocate. Did he want her to look after his sister or not? The most upsetting thing was that it made her realise just how much she had been allowing him to guide her in the decision, putting her desire to leave the nurses' home and her pleasure at Dr Entwistle's recommendation very much in second place.

I won't accept the job because of Tom Russell, she

thought feverishly, and not for the first time. He's completely irrelevant to my life, and he always will be.

She made the mistake of looking at him as the thought formed in her mind, and had to suppress a gasp of awareness as she met his gaze. His mouth, sober just a minute ago, had drifted into a lazy smile, and she wanted to taste those freckles on his nose with her tongue.

'Can I. . .go for a walk in the garden while I think it over?' she blurted, and brother and sister looked at each other.

'Of course, sweetie,' Faye said. 'Open the lattice door for her, would you, Tom? It's a bit stiff.'

'I can manage,' said Belinda, darting towards the safety of shrubs and shade that beckoned her, but he came up behind her as she struggled with the iron latch and she felt his breath fan the tiny hairs on the nape of her neck. Then a large warm hand clamped over her own fumbling fingers and gently removed them so that he could work the latch. The door swung smoothly open, and she almost ran down the wooden steps in her white sandals, out of the magic circle of masculine arms that had almost enclosed her.

She found a jasmine-scented corner of garden at the side of the house and sat down on a rustic wooden seat, watching twittering birds come and go fearlessly around a hanging seed basket. She could still hear the faint murmurs of Tom Russell and his sister talking on the veranda, and it distracted her from the real purpose of this time alone, which was *not* to go on reliving that moment when his hand had covered her own, but to obediently follow his suggestion of giving herself time to fully think this through.

Restlessly, she rose again and continued on around the house, following a cool stone path that seemed to be sloping down through the lush growth of shrubs and trees. She was almost on top of the river before she realised that this was where the path was leading, and here she found another seat from which she could see a boat or two plaiting lazy fans of rippling wake through the smooth water.

This place was like the garden of Eden, she thought whimsically, and she didn't know if the job here was a serpent's temptation or a golden apple. No, that was a stupid comparison. If it weren't for Dr Russell, the decision would be easy. . .

'*Here* you are!' he said behind her. 'I've been beating the bushes looking for you for hours!' He was exaggerating, of course, but all the same, she must have been away for longer than she had intended.

'Made up your mind?' he asked gently.

'I. . . I don't know.' She stood up, hating her own weakness, and he stepped forward so that he was directly in front of her, frowning down at her troubled face.

'You're not looking very relaxed, love,' he said.

'Oh. . .yes, I am.'

'No. Your shoulders are pulled up as tightly as a drawn bow.' He reached towards her with his strong hands and pressed them down on the fine-boned structure of her shoulders, massaging with rhythmic, kneading movements. 'I've pressured you into this the whole way, haven't I?' he murmured. 'I'm sorry. Let's go back and tell Faye to go back to the nursing agency with a more open mind.'

'Perhaps that would be best,' she answered at last, after a long pause. His hands dropped from her shoulders, and he did not speak, merely took her hand and pulled her after him, striding back up the path at a rapid pace so that she was hard pressed to keep up.

He must have taken a short cut that she hadn't noticed on her way down, as they arrived back at the house sooner than she was expecting and went straight to the veranda, where Faye still lay on the lounger, enjoying a long drink of iced water. Tom flung himself back into the chair beside her, still without speaking, and Belinda stood there while Faye gave her a watchful glance.

'Well?' she said, pressing long, sensitive fingers into her lightly freckled forehead. 'Is there a decision?'

'Yes,' Belinda nodded. She saw the tension and fear that was putting lines of stress around the other woman's eyes and mouth and squeezing her hands into tight, pale fists. The healing power of Dr Russell's earlier reassurance had ebbed, it seemed. Hardly surprising. Diabetes and its complications could be serious and life-threatening, both to mother and baby. Faye had had two miscarriages and now a threat hung over this pregnancy as well. A silly, immature crush on Faye's brother suddenly seemed very trivial by comparison.

'I *will* take the job. I'll start as soon as I can,' she promised suddenly, knowing as the words were spoken that they sealed her decision once and for all.

Tom Russell glanced up at her quickly, surprise, relief and approval clearly visible in those symmetrically drawn features. He had deliberately withdrawn his insistence at the last minute, Belinda realised now, so that her decision came freely.

'In that case,' he said, at once lazily in control, 'I think we should be able to wangle it so that you can start tomorrow.'

CHAPTER THREE

'THIS is Mrs Hamilton's case-file,' said Dr Owen Greene, dumping a hefty wad of papers into Belinda's hands.

'My goodness!' she murmured. 'It's enormous!'

'Yes, and it's going to get bigger,' said the senior consultant in obstetrics at Coronation Hospital.

Belinda had been slightly unnerved to find that this man was Faye Hamilton's obstetrician, and was rather alarmed at the prospect of spending a block of time in his elegant office, becoming familiar with the case history of her new patient.

'Would you like me just to look through it all?' she offered. 'Or do you have time to explain some of her problems yourself?'

'I have time,' he nodded, leaning back. 'And if I didn't, I'd *make* time. Bill Hamilton was the architect and building contractor for the new wing here eight years ago, and he's about to get to work on a completely new building for obstetrics and gynaecology. What's more, he's on the board of the university where I teach. I'd like to think that I never give *poor* care to any patient for political reasons,' he mused somewhat pompously, 'but I'm certainly not above giving extra *good* care to the wife of an important man like Bill!'

'Of course,' Belinda murmured, thinking that it was typical of Dr Russell not to mention this illustrious connection, which she found a little intimidating.

Then she wondered suddenly if Tom Russell had *known* she would find it intimidating and had deliberately kept her in the dark. That sort of protectiveness would be typical of him, she decided, and felt a small, perverse spurt of anger. She would have to show him that she wasn't quite as helpless and unworldly as he seemed to think!

'So Dr Russell is professionally involved in his sister's case as an endocrine specialist?' she went on quickly.

'Yes, we're consulting quite closely,' Dr Greene nodded, his swivel chair creaking importantly as he rocked his rather bulky body slowly back and forth. 'And of course he's very much involved personally, because he's close to Faye and he's concerned. We all are.' His sweeping gesture seemed to suggest that 'we' was a very large group of people indeed. 'She's a fascinating person and a wonderful painter, and this baby is very important to her.'

'She's a painter?' Belinda queried.

'You haven't heard of her? Faye Russell? She paints under her maiden name,' he added helpfully, but Belinda was still forced to shake her head.

'I'm sorry. . .'

'My goodness!' He was struck silent for quite some seconds, as if ignorance of Faye Russell's work was on a par with believing that the earth was flat. Then he rallied and said, 'Well, you're in for a treat, in that case, surrounded by her paintings in that lovely house. I'm sure you'll become a fan.'

'I'm sure I will,' she agreed.

'Meanwhile, you need to know more about her case.'

'Yes. I understand she's already had two miscarriages?'

They spent nearly an hour discussing Faye Hamilton's obstetrical and gynaecological history, and at the end of it Belinda was reeling. She had read that to be an artist it was necessary to have known personal suffering, and, while she was rather sceptical of this idea, if there *was* any truth in it, then Faye ought to be on her way to the status of a Michelangelo.

For several years she had suffered from painful endometriosis, which was at first misdiagnosed and then treated unnecessarily by surgery. 'Only after the endometrial tissue grew back did she come to *me*.' Dr Greene informed Belinda smugly. 'I treated it with a three-month course of Danocrine, followed by surgery which *was* necessary by this time, but was only effective and permanent because of the follow-up Danocrine treatment.'

Then, as soon as this treatment had finished, Faye had become unknowingly pregnant, and had only discovered the fact through the onset of a painful and debilitating miscarriage.

'She was a very heavy smoker at that stage,' Dr Greene explained, his disapproval very clear. 'Over two packs a day, very foolish for a diabetic, but she hadn't come to terms with the illness at that stage, and was quite defiant about a number of things, Professor Rankin tells me.' Belinda nodded slowly, recognising the name of one of the country's most illustrious specialists in diabetes, now working in Sydney. 'As well, of course, we now know that there's a very direct link between the amount a woman smokes and her chance of miscarrying. If Mrs Hamilton had realised that she was pregnant, she would have stopped smoking, and in fact she did stop after the miscarriage.'

'And the second miscarriage?'

'Related to her diabetes. It was a planned pregnancy, and she'd been working hard at getting her blood sugar under control, but that often can't be done overnight.'

'No, and it needs time and discipline as well as motivation,' Belinda murmured, the instinctive empathy she had felt for Faye growing as she heard more of the painter's story.

'Indeed,' he agreed, seeming a little irritated by her interruption, as if, as when he was giving a lecture, he preferred to hold the floor.

Belinda bit her lip. In the normal course of her work at Coronation Hospital, she would never come into such personal contact with a man as important as Dr Greene, and she would have to remember that he wanted her to recognise this fact while she was Faye Hamilton's nurse. Thank goodness Dr Russell wasn't quite so unapproachable!

But this was a dangerous way to look at it. Professionally Tom Russell might be commendably egalitarian, but personally he was as far out of her league as ever. What was Dr Greene saying now, though?

'Now the fact that Mrs Hamilton is diabetic isn't generally known, Sister Jones, and Mrs Hamilton doesn't want it to be. Your discretion in the matter is, of course, understood.'

'Of course,' she agreed.

'That's another reason, I gather, why the selection of a nurse has been difficult. Mrs Hamilton wasn't confident that the agency nurses she interviewed would respect her desire for confidentiality on the subject. I haven't involved myself in the problem,' he said dismissively with a sweep of his pinkly scrubbed hand. 'My advice was that she spend the duration of her pregnancy in hospital.'

'Because of the diabetes?'

'That and other factors,' he answered. 'A first episode of bleeding several weeks ago led to a thyroid function test, and we found that to be a little low, so that's now being treated medicinally. Then a sonogram this morning revealed that she has a degree of placenta praevia—the past heavy smoking is a factor there again, I'm afraid. It's only partial, fortunately, but that may change. The bleeding she's experiencing now is caused by the condition. She hasn't yet been told what I saw on the sonogram by the way. I wanted to wait until the pictures were developed and until I could make a written report.'

'I understand. I won't say anything until——'

'Dr Russell will talk it over with her tonight, show her the sonogram pictures, and I think it'll convince her that the bed-rest really is necessary. She may even concede that hospitalisation is best, at least for the last trimester. But with you on board ensuring that she rests and manages her insulin. . .'

'That blood-sugar level is the really crucial thing, isn't it?' said Belinda.

'Yes, so even though she's been on a self-monitoring programme for several years now I felt that constant professional supervision was necessary, and so did Dr Russell.'

There was a knock at the door, and the consultant obstetrician growled an imperative, 'Come in!'

Belinda knew it would be Tom Russell, but that didn't stop her from flushing foolishly at the sight of him standing in the doorway, jiggling his car keys in his hand. He had come, as arranged, to take her and her belongings over to the Hamiltons'.

'Finished?' he asked, and Belinda turned questioningly to Dr Greene.

'Yes, we're finished,' he nodded. 'And I think Miss Jones is feeling somewhat daunted. Faye won't reconsider the hospital stay?'

'Not at this stage, certainly,' Faye's brother answered confidently. '*Are* you feeling daunted, Belinda?'

'Well, if *I* am, Mrs Hamilton certainly must be,' she

told him seriously, not wanting either of the doctors to see that she did indeed find the responsibility she was about to take on quite daunting now that she knew the full scope of Faye Hamilton's problems.

The dynamic painter was going against her own doctor's advice by remaining at home, and a busy man like Dr Greene, although willing to extend the level of his professional care, could not provide the constant medical supervision available at a big hospital like Coronation. So she was inexpressibly relieved when Tom Russell said, 'And since *I'm* daunted by Faye's problems as well, I'll be visiting almost every day.'

The relief must have shown in her face, as she caught his brief little smile of amusement drifting in her direction, and when she thought back on their encounters lately she realised that he often seemed to glance at her in that same lightly amused way, as if he found her mildly diverting—the way he might feel, perhaps, about a pretty child. Somehow she did not find the comparison flattering, and with two spots of sudden colour in her cheeks she drew herself upright and thrust out her firm but fine-boned chin.

'Dr Greene must be busy, Dr Russell. I think if I can look at these notes until tomorrow,' she looked questioningly at Dr Greene, who nodded, 'I needn't take up any more of his time now.'

'That's very good, Belinda,' Tom Russell answered mildly, 'but I have a couple of other matters to discuss with him, concerning another diabetic patient. I'll only be five minutes. Would you mind waiting outside?'

'Of course not,' she said quickly, already on her way out of the room and feeling that her attempt at asserting herself had not been a success. Probably it had been foolish to try to do so. As Faye's private nurse, she would be filling an important position, and

her professionalism or lack of it could make the difference between a healthy baby and another tragic loss.
Still, these men held the lives of mothers and unborn
babies in their hands like this every day. Perched on
the edge of an upholstered beige chair outside Dr
Greene's office, she felt small and insignificant and
extremely chastened.

It must have showed—or else Tom Russell was
already far too skilled at reading her emotions—
because his first words to her when they were seated in
his red sports car were, 'Cat got your tongue?'

'No,' she answered in a small voice. 'I just. . .don't
have anything to say.'

'Really? And for that reason you're actually not
saying it. What delightfully rare discrimination!'

'Oh!' she bleated, her voice high and rather indig-
nant. 'What do you. . .?'

He laughed. 'Do I seem to be teasing? Perhaps I do.
But I'm serious. With so many of the women I know—
and the men, for that matter—the less they have to
say, the more they talk. I find it maddening.'

'Yes, I suppose it must be,' she agreed.

They had left the hospital grounds now, and she
thought about the two suitcases in the back of the car.
It hadn't taken her long to clear out her room at the
nurses' home this morning, and her father had come
over at lunch to take several boxes of things back to
his suburban home for storage. The two suitcases
represented everything she thought she would need for
the next seven months at the Hamiltons', and it seemed
like an odd way to be taking what might be a big step
in her life.

She was taking eight months' leave without pay from
Coronation, but in the back of her mind was the odd
feeling that she wouldn't be going back, and she didn't

quite know what it meant. She was still pondering this, as well as thinking about Faye Hamilton and the long difficult journey through pregnancy that lay ahead, when she became aware that Dr Russell was laughing to himself—just a quiet chuckle at first, but as he realised she was watching him and saw her bemused expression the sound grew to a full-throated and resonant guffaw.

'What *is* it?' she squeaked.

'You,' he managed, drawing breath with difficulty.

'Me?'

'Yes! I just gave you an extremely provocative conversational opening, and you murmured a polite nothing and let it lapse.'

'Oh, I'm sorry. Did you want to . . .to discuss it?'

He was still laughing. 'Actually, I thought I didn't. I thought I'd be relieved that you didn't have to pick my comment apart and use it as an opening for deep amateur psychoanalysis of *myself, yourself*, and half a dozen other people as well! But then, when you didn't say anything at all, I found I was disappointed.'

'So you've learnt something, haven't you?' she retorted, daring to put some spice into it, since she felt somewhat persecuted by his teasing manner. Again, she felt she was only entertaining him as he might have been entertained by a clever child.

'Have I?' he asked now. 'And what's that?'

'That you're thoroughly contrary!'

'Hmm. . . So this *is* turning into amateur analysis, is it?'

'Only because you steered it that way,' Belinda said crossly.

'True, he mused. 'Perhaps we were better off with silence.'

'I think we were!'

And then he discomfited her utterly by keeping that silence until he had turned into the Hamiltons' driveway, switched off the engine, and opened the boot to retrieve her luggage.

'Now,' he said at last, hefting a suitcase in each hand without apparent effort, 'can I leave you to unpack while I talk to Faye?'

'Of course. Dr Greene said you'll be telling her the result of the sonogram.'

'Yes, which may upset her, as you can imagine, although at least it fully accounts for the bleeding. So I've brought something which I hope will give her good news as well. Here, can you bring it in for me?'

He put her suitcases down in the driveway and reached into the boot to pass her a carry-case which Belinda recognised as containing a portable monitor, something like an electrically amplified stethoscope, which meant that it was often possible for a pregnant woman to hear her baby's heartbeat as early as ten weeks into the pregnancy.

'It could backfire, of course,' Dr Russell said as they walked towards the front steps together. 'She's only eleven weeks, and I'm not an obstetrician, so my experience with doing this is a little rusty. If she can't hear the heart she may get frightened, but there's a good chance, so I'm going to take the risk. What's the time, by the way? My watch is running slow.'

'Half-past five.'

'Good! Bill should be home soon, and he'll be able to hear it too.'

Faye was lying on the outdoor lounger on the veranda as she had been yesterday, and she greeted Belinda briefly, her face creased with tension, before turning to Tom. 'Dr Greene has deputised you to show me the sonogram pictures and explain them, I hope.'

Her tone betrayed the fact that she had been keyed up about it ever since the procedure had been done this morning at the obstetrician's consulting-rooms, and Belinda hoped Faye had been keeping careful tabs on her blood-sugar level in case it was being affected by her mood.

'Can I get to my room round this way?' asked Belinda quickly as she slid her suitcases from Tom's grasp and began to walk to the corner of the veranda which led around to the side of the house.

'Yes, please make yourself at home,' Faye answered, but her politeness was mechanical, and Belinda suppressed a grunt of effort as she lifted the cases. She didn't want Dr Russell to feel he had to help her with her luggage when it was so obvious that he and Faye wanted to talk privately about the sonogram.

The room, reached this time from the veranda, was just as lovely as she had remembered, and after folding some clothes neatly in drawers and hanging the rest on satin-padded hangers in the wardrobe she fussed for quite some time with the scanty collection of knick-knacks she had brought, trying to arrange them so that they harmonised with the tranquil simplicity of the décor.

Lastly she went to hang her towel and arrange her toiletries in the bathroom, only to find several thick towels of varying sizes already hanging there for her use, and an array of soaps, lotions and hygiene products that made her own cheaply bought things seem scarcely worthy of being unpacked.

Impulsively, and without changing from the pale blue uniform she had put on this morning, since she didn't know how Faye wanted her new nurse to dress, Belinda found her way to the kitchen where the housekeeper, Mrs Porter, was creating deliciously savoury aromas as she cooked a three-course evening meal that was carefully balanced with Faye's special needs in mind.

'Did you arrange all those lovely things in my bathroom?' she asked at once, before an attack of shyness could take hold of her.

'Yes,' Mrs Porter nodded, 'but don't thank me for it—it was Mrs Hamilton's idea. She thought you'd probably never had a bathroom to yourself and that you'd appreciate something a bit special.'

'Oh, wasn't that nice of her?'

'She has a heart of gold,' Mrs Porter said decisively, then added, 'Which is a good thing, actually, because if she didn't I wouldn't stay! She's very difficult to work for on her creative days!'

'Is she? Mmm. . .' Dr Russell had hinted at Faye's artistic temperament as well. 'But I don't suppose she'll be doing much painting while I'm here.'

A rather cryptic snort was the only response to this, as Mrs Porter turned to stir her soup, and Belinda, seeing that the housekeeper was too busy for chat, wondered what to do next. Mrs Porter herself answered the question a few moments later.

'If you're going to join them on the veranda,' she said, 'I've just made coffee. If it's not too much trouble you can add a cup for yourself and take it out.'

'Of course! It's no trouble at all.' The housekeeper's request answered Belinda's doubt that brother and sister might not yet be ready for an intrusion, and after adding a fourth almost transparent bone-china coffee-cup and saucer to the engraved silver tray, she carried it carefully through the series of open, interconnected rooms until she reached the veranda.

She heard voices as soon as she opened the glass-panelled door, and had already been warned by the four cups that Faye's husband must be home. He rose from a cushioned wicker chair as soon as he saw her and came to take the tray, saying, 'You're Belinda, of course. I'm Bill. I'm so glad you've come to help us out.'

He was a tall man—not quite as tall as Tom Russell, but still over six feet—with slightly thinning hair that had once been a dark brown but was now streaked with grey. He must be in his early forties, Belinda decided, while Faye, she knew was thirty-eight—fairly old to be having a first child, which added a greater sense of urgency and importance to the task of keeping her pregnancy on track.

'Belinda!' Tom Russell held out his car keys and tossed them to her. The throw took her by surprise, was sharp and strong, and went a little wide, so that it was only the experience of three younger brothers that gave her quick enough reflexes to shoot an arm out sideways to take the catch. She caught the raised eyebrow and quirked corner of his mouth as he said, 'I'm impressed!' and couldn't help smiling smugly. 'Can you go down to the car and bring up my medical bag?' his question explained the keys. 'There's some gel in there that we need before we can try to find that heartbeat.'

'OK,' she nodded quickly, and noticed as she left the veranda that Bill Hamilton had moved closer to his wife's side and engulfed her slim artist's hand in his larger, stronger one in a gesture of silent support. Faye hadn't spoken since Belinda joined the group, and her stylishly applied make-up couldn't conceal the tear-stains on her face. Her brother's explanation of what the sonogram had revealed had understandably upset her—yet another complication!

Dr Russell had set up the monitor when Belinda

returned. It was a simple piece of equipment that could be plugged into an ordinary power socket, and Faye had been happy to remain where she was. Her loose silk smock had been raised, while the elastic waistband of her matching trousers had been lowered a few inches so that her pale abdomen, not yet beginning to swell with the new life inside her, was ready to be smeared lightly with the gel that would facilitate the task of finding the tiny heartbeat.

No one had poured coffee yet, and the silence on the veranda was now very tense. Tom pressed the stethoscope-like circle of metal lightly on Faye's abdomen, waited a moment, moved it slightly, and waited again. A loud, rather slow thudding drew a questioning glance from Bill Hamilton, but Tom shook his head. 'That's Faye's,' he said. 'The baby's will be much faster and fainter.'

He moved the instrument again and the sound of Faye's heartbeat changed a little, but was still the only rhythmic sound. 'It's early days yet,' said Tom, the cheerfulness in his manner a little forced. 'We'll try again next——' Then he broke off, made a tiny adjustment of the device, and suddenly there it was—a rapid, fluttering little beat that was lost again for several seconds as Faye tensed and moved.

When it came into focus once more—the unmistakable beat of a new life, amplified by modern technology—Faye's face spread in the widest smile Belinda had ever seen. At the same time, tears coursed heedlessly down her cheeks and Bill, at her side, grinned as well.

'There's a baby. There *is* a baby!' Faye gasped. 'I. . . I can't believe it! I didn't believe it before, and now. . .'

'It's a baby all right,' Tom agreed. 'And that's a beautiful strong beat.'

'You're there! You're really there!' Faye touched a hand to her abdomen, not caring about the smear of clear, odourless gel there, and the slight movement made the heartbeat disappear again. 'Find it, Tom!' she ordered firmly. 'I know I can't go on listening to it all day, but find it one more time.'

After a short search, he had positioned the listening instrument in the right spot for the third time, and the rapid beat of sound came again. 'Will you bring that contraption with you every time you come, Tom, please?' she begged.

'Every time?' he queried.

'Once a week, then. I haven't felt this happy since— I don't know! Oh, Bill!'

Faye turned and buried her face in her husband's shoulder, and Belinda's throat constricted suddenly as she saw how their love for each other and their concern for the tiny life growing inside Faye united them in both happiness and fear. A little embarrassed at trespassing on this very private moment between them, she found a pack of tissues in Dr Russell's medical bag and handed them to him so that Faye could wipe the gel from her abdomen before adjusting her clothing again.

Next, while the endocrine specialist packed his equipment away, she poured coffee for everyone, and carefully committed Faye's preference of black with no sugar to memory. She was pleased that Faye drank it that way, since without food value it wouldn't affect her blood sugar level or insulin intake and therefore didn't have to be regulated in quantity and timing. Tom Russell, she learned at the same time, drank his black as well.

The next ten minutes passed in general conversation, as Bill Hamilton asked Belinda about herself, while she in turn heard more about his very successful work as an architect and building contractor. Only after a silence had fallen did she turn to Faye.

'And I only found out this morning from Dr Greene what a. . .a. . . ' she couldn't think of a suitable word and said finally, '. . .*celebrated* painter you are.'

'A *celebrated* painter,' Faye echoed with an amused smile, so that Belinda wondered if she should have said, 'well-known' instead. 'I suppose I am. I certainly feel like celebra*ting* my painting at the moment—I haven't done any for weeks. Tom, can I. . .?'

'Can you paint lying on the couch?' he growled.

'I'll have to, won't I? Starting tomorrow. Lord, I can't wait!'

'And what sort of things will be you painting?' Belinda asked politely, feeling that she was venturing into quite unknown—but surely fairly safe?—conversational territory.

'You!' was the startling reply.

'Me?' Belinda echoed hollowly, as Dr Russell interrupted her.

'Now listen, Faye——' Both women turned to him in surprise. His anger was sudden and strong.

'Well, Tom, Really!' Faye answered him impatiently, taking his flashing blue eyes completely in her stride, although they had given Belinda a rush of nervous warmth. 'You know I almost always have female figures in my work. I'm not suddenly going to start painting bowls of fruit. Although perhaps Belinda *with* a bowl of fruit. . .'

'Faye. . .' Tom began.

'Otherwise what's she going to do with her time, poor girl? She can't spend *all* day monitoring my blood sugar and giving me my thyroid medicine, and if I can't paint I shall go mad!'

But her vibrant, reasoned tone seemed to slip off him without any effect at all. He had got restlessly to his feet and was leaning over the green wooden railing that came to waist height at the edge of the veranda, but after a suppressed exclamation he wheeled to face his sister again. 'Hasn't it occurred to you to ask Belinda's permission? It wasn't in the job description, you know.'

'All right,' Faye returned, suddenly appearing to capitulate. 'Bill, the budget can run to an artist's model as well, can it?'

'If you want it to,' he answered simply, a rock of reasonableness that Belinda found rather reassuring in the sea of emotion between brother and sister.

'You're missing the point, Faye,' Tom Russell growled.

'Am I? What *is* the point?'

'Simply that you should have asked Belinda instead of just making assumptions. It would have been more polite.'

'Speaking of manners,' Belinda herself put in suddenly, in a rather small but very firm voice, '*I* think it would be polite if you *both* stopped speaking about me as if I wasn't here!'

Brother and sister, suddenly looking very much alike, turned with surprised faces to the blonde nurse, and she flushed, her brief confidence wilting under the twin blue gazes. They *weren't* twins, but they could have been in some respects, she realised. Clearly they both enjoyed a good row together.

'Sorry, Belinda.' Tom was the first to speak, very gruffly. 'You're right. Faye and I are playing family feud—it's an old favourite of ours—and you're piggy in the middle. What *do* you think about Faye using you as a model?'

'Well, it would seem a better idea than engaging a model,' she answered seriously. 'There'll be a lot of interruptions. I'll be monitoring her blood-sugar level pretty frequently, won't I? There's a lot of fatigue in pregnancy, and a model might have to wait around with nothing to do. Since I'll be on call anyway, it would seem more sensible for me to fill both roles.'

'Yes, that makes sense from Faye's point of view,' Tom agreed impatiently. 'But how do *you* feel?'

Belinda met his searching gaze for several seconds, then answered simply, 'I don't know. I've never been painted before.'

And she wasn't really surprised when he threw back his head and laughed.

CHAPTER FOUR

'So HOW did it go today?' Tom Russell asked two days later.

'Good,' Belinda nodded, taking it as a polite enquiry that didn't require a detailed response.

At Dr Russell's request. . .no, not Dr Russell. She was to call him Tom from now on, he had said. . .she had walked him to his car after he had dropped in to see Faye over lunch. The latter was having a nap now, which Belinda was pleased about, as she suspected that the dynamic painter might well try to fight fatigue in the future when a painting session was going well. If the routine of a nap got well established now, then it would be easier to keep it in place later on, when Faye was in the second trimester and feeling deceptively fit and healthy as women usually did in those middle months. . .

But Dr Russell. . .*Tom*. . .hadn't got into his car as she had expected him to do. What was he saying?

'More detail than that, Belinda, please.'

'Oh! Well, as Faye told you over lunch, she feels that her morning sickness is beginning to taper off. And when Dr Greene examined her this morning he said the placental bleeding had completely stopped. You saw how happy she was about that. She had a blood sugar reading of a hundred and sixty yesterday afternoon, and we realised that with the lighter schedule her morning component of NPH insulin will have to be raised. You'd probably like to check on that for us.'

54

'Yes, I would. And as her pregnancy advances her need for insulin will gradually increase. There'll be some fine tuning involved all the way along. Have you looked at the daily chart she fills in that records all those details?' asked Tom.

'Yes, we've decided to do the chart together,' Belinda answered, looking up an impossibly long way to meet his blue gaze as she spoke. 'That way she's still fully aware of what's happening to her blood sugar and why, and I'm learning more about her individual reactions, as well as providing an extra check. There's always a chance that one of us will miss a telltale pattern or a problem somewhere.'

'Sounds sensible to me.'

He questioned her in more detail for several more minutes, asking about sleep, moods, energy levels and half a dozen other tiny things that revealed his deep concern for his sister. Belinda relaxed unconsciously as she gave the detailed answers he wanted, reassured by the way he seemed to trust what she said. Not all doctors *did* trust nurses, she had found, and it was something that always made her timid and hesitant.

Then, just when she was feeling really at ease with him, he stepped back a pace, came in on the tail-end of her report on the new extra-calorie meal schedule they were working on, and undermined her equilibrium totally with the words, 'I like the way the dappled light is playing on your hair. In sunshine it's really blonde. I hadn't noticed before.' Then, before she could reply at all, 'Which reminds me—how's life as an artist's model?'

'Oh, it's—well, it's fine. Working on her art doesn't seem to be tiring Faye at all, and——'

'Not Faye, love! I'm not asking about her. How are

you enjoying being turned into some blobs of pink and mauve on a canvas?'

Blobs!

'Well, so far she's just sketching with pencil or Conte stick.' Belinda tried to bring out the new artist's term nonchalantly, but he wasn't fooled.

'Conte stick? All right. And is it chiaroscuro or pentimento?'

'Oh, I don't know.' She flushed and looked down, feeling he had exposed her ignorance cruelly. Those Italian-sounding words meant nothing to her, and he must know it. 'Faye didn't say.'

Her voice trailed away completely as he reached lazily towards her with a long arm. 'Belinda Jones, am I a beast?' The words were spoken as his hand touched her shoulder and slid around her back, drawing her into the warm sheltering cliff of his chest.

'Yes,' she said tremulously against him, feeling her flesh melt off her bones into puddles of helpless weakness on the ground.

'I'm not really, you know,' he insisted gently, resting his chin lightly on her hair. The words seemed to vibrate against the softness of her cotton-clad flesh, which was in such disturbing contact with his musk-scented blue shirt. 'Can't you stand a little teasing?'

'Of course I can,' she answered, making it very firm. 'We tease each other all the time at home. But teasing shouldn't contain too much truth or it isn't teasing any more, it's. . .it's. . .'

'Bullying?' he suggested, his mouth, with its full, sensitive upper lip, very serious now. He still held her, and, although she wanted to step back from his light, casual embrace in order to regain strength in her limbs, her legs wouldn't obey her brain's command to move.

'No, not bullying,' she said. Ironically, she wanted

to defend him now. The word was too harsh. 'It's just—just dampening, that's all. You teased me because you thought I was ignorant, and you were right. I don't know what those words mean. I've never studied art. I've studied nursing, I work hard at it and I think I'm good at it. I'm proud of that, but——'

'Hey!' A cool firm finger against her lips stemmed her confused tide of words. 'I'm sorry, but can we get one thing straight? I *don't* think you're ignorant. . .not in any negative sense, anyway. I find it refreshing that you don't talk in the same artsy, pretentious way as some of my sister's friends—and *my* friends too, if I'm honest. Coming from me, teasing is a backhanded compliment, and you'd better get used to the idea.'

'Had I? All right,' she said obediently, deciding to take it as a professional instruction.

Tom laughed, of course, and she didn't know if she was pleased or angered that he so often seemed to find her so amusing. But at least he had released her from that disturbing contact with his wide, strong chest and firm encircling arms, and the physical contact between them had brought one thing home to her very clearly— such a thing must definitely not happen again, or these next months would be utterly impossible.

For a moment she thought she would find the courage to say something about it, but then she realised that the timing was all wrong. He had shrugged off the personal tone of their conversation now with an impatient glance at his watch.

'Heavens—twenty-five past two, and I'm due at the hospital by half past. Why is it that lately I always seem to get caught up in. . .?' But he didn't finish the sentence, adding instead an irritable, 'Never mind! I'll see you tomorrow.'

'Will you? All right.' Belinda spoke as neutrally as possible. Too neutrally, it seemed.

'Don't sound so pleased!' The teasing tone was back and he flicked a finger lightly against her cheek. 'Or I won't come to the party.'

'*Party*?' she echoed.

'Yes, didn't Faye tell you? Not a *party*, I suppose, but she and Bill are having some people over tomorrow evening, and I'm one of them.'

'Oh.'

'And now I *must* go!'

He did, sliding fluidly into the driver's seat of the red sports car and reversing expertly out of the driveway while she was still trying to recover from that last lightly sarcastic comment.

Staring helplessly after the departing vehicle, she felt a light breeze cooling the mist of perspiration that had dampened her temples, and the fine peacock-blue cotton of her full skirt—Faye had decreed 'no uniform'—flared and dropped again, caressing her bare legs like the teasing touch of a man's fingers. The lush tropical foliage overhead moved, creating lilting patterns of light, and she remembered what Tom Russell had said about her hair.

Knowing that she simply *had* to shake off this mood of dreamy awareness, she turned on her heel, some grit beneath the leather soles of her flat white sandals grating harshly. Faye would be awake again soon. She was due for a snack at three, followed by another blood-sugar reading, and Belinda had planned to spend the time until then reading up on some aspects of prenatal care that she felt hazy on.

As well, Faye had asked earlier if they could devote some time to foot care, which both knew was very important. All diabetics had to take extra care with their feet, and pregnancy only increased the risk of problems related to poor circulation.

Thank goodness for nursing! Belinda thought as she hurried up the front steps. With so much to do and think about, she would have forgotten about Tom Russell altogether in another few minutes—she hoped.

'That's lovely, Belinda!' Faye Hamilton smiled. 'Just like that! Do you think you can hold it for an hour?'

'Yes, I hope so,' Belinda answered uncertainly.

'Hmm. Perhaps it's too hard for you. . .'

'No.'

'But I love the pose. How about a short break in half an hour?'

'Yes, that would be better, I think,' Belinda admitted.

She was dressed in a white silk slip belonging to Faye and sitting on the dark wooden floor of the veranda, leaning her arms on a white wicker chair. Behind her was the backdrop of green garden foliage, and just out of her reach, on a small coffee-table that she had positioned at Faye's instruction, stood an enormous vase filled with flowers—all red ones, ranging from deepest crimson to a vibrant vermilion orange. After sketching her many times over the past two days in all sorts of positions, and studying the sketches for an hour earlier this morning, Faye was now ready to paint.

'Belinda, love, can you remember exactly how you are, and go and get your brush and brush your hair round so that it lies spread out on the chair?' she said.

'Of course.' Belinda rose obediently and was back in a minute or two, then the posing began in earnest and there was silence on the veranda as Faye worked and Belinda waited. Time seemed to go rather slowly at first. Belinda watched a triangular patch of sunlight creep across the far end of the veranda. It shrank steadily as the sun rose towards its zenith. She heard the drone of some bees in the garden and the angry chatter of birds disputing over their seeds.

I'd love to have a beautiful garden one day, she thought idly. She began to landscape the fantasy garden in her mind and had soon forgotten about the slight ache in her hips that came from having her legs curled to one side, and the uncomfortable weave of the wickerwork pressing into the soft skin on the underside of her forearms.

By the time masculine footsteps sounded on the flight of steps beyond the veranda, she couldn't have said whether twenty minutes had passed or fifty. But she knew immediately who the footsteps belonged to, and she knew also that she was blushing. All at once the pose for Faye seemed like a prison as she felt the heat and colour creep up her neck and face, and she jumped self-consciously as Faye said, 'Damn! That wash of colour isn't right.'

But of course Faye wasn't referring to the colour on her face.

'No, it's too pale,' said Tom, coming up behind his sister and studying her canvas.

'You're here early,' Faye accused, putting her brush tip-upwards in a jar.

'Am I? It's ten past twelve. I came from the university—had a guest lecture to give.'

'Ten past twelve!' Belinda exclaimed, horrified. She was desperate to move now, physical awareness returning suddenly to her body and making her realise that she was numb in her left leg and stiff everywhere else. Faye had started painting her at eleven and was supposed to have had a blood glucose test at noon.

'I lost track of time,' Faye admitted ruefully. 'Get up, Belinda, and have a stretch.'

Belinda didn't need to be told twice. Tom was staring at her accusingly, and she wanted to hurry to get the glucose testing kit at once, but on her first stride the numb leg gave way beneath her and she staggered clumsily until she felt his hands steady her with a firm grip on each forearm.

Belinda was instantly aware of the fact that she was dressed only in the silk slip that Faye had decided best captured the mood she wanted for her painting. She had her underclothing beneath, of course, and the expensive silk was of such a luxuriously close weave that there was nothing immodest about the outfit. In fact, a recent flip through Faye's pile of fashion magazines told Belinda that simple spaghetti-strapped dresses modelled on the design of slips were now the height of fashion for evening wear in New York and Paris. None the less, the short skirt and fragile straps revealed more of her pale, honey-gold skin than she felt happy with.

As he held her from behind, Tom's hips and thighs were solid against the thinly covered curves of her lower torso, and as usual the contact between them made her immediately weak and speechless.

Tom, however, was not speechless at all. 'My God, what's happened to your arms?' he rasped, turning her expertly with a spin of her slim shoulders and lifting her right hand to expose the pale, tender skin of her forearm. She followed his angry gaze and saw the pattern of the wicker weave pressed into dark red bas-relief.

'It's all right,' she blurted. 'It'll go away in an hour. It's just a bit red.'

'A bit red! Faye, how long did you have her in that

pose?' He released her as suddenly as he had come to her support and she grasped quickly and covertly at the back of another chair, not wanting him to know that her numbed leg was tingling painfully now.

'Oh, Tom, I lost track of time,' Faye said again.'Belinda, love, why didn't you say something?'

'I. . . I suppose I lost track of time too,' Belinda explained lamely, too consumed with riding out the worst of the tingling as feeling returned to her leg. 'I'd better get the glucose testing kit,' she mumbled as she edged towards the French window that led into the breakfast-room and then along a passage to the suite of rooms used by Faye and Bill. Faye's medical supplies were kept there in a large lockable cupboard, and that blood-sugar level should be monitored within the next ten minutes.

Once inside the door, however, she found that her leg was still too stiff and tingling to move properly, so she sat down in one of the pale, bentwood breakfast chairs. . . Ah, the relief!

But the sudden sense of comfort was short lived. Outside on the veranda, after a brief, uncomfortable silence, Belinda heard the low, threatening rumble of Tom's voice. 'For God's sake, Faye, I know you're an artist, but have some consideration!'

'She could have said something,' Faye hedged.

They were both speaking in the slightly lowered tone that meant they did not want to be overheard, and were only having the discussion at all because they believed Belinda to be safely out of earshot. Hating to eavesdrop, Belinda struggled to her feet again as Tom spoke. 'You know she's far too intimidated by you to do that!'

'Intimidated? By me? She's not!' Faye protested.

'All right, perhaps not by you personally, but by

your status as an artist, she certainly is. Put yourself in her place, Faye! She's got to put up with you for the next six months or more!'

'Oh, and I'm such an ogre! Really, Tom, the way you're defending her, anyone would think I'd tortured the girl! She can have a clock in view from now on, so we don't go beyond half an hour at a time. But I think you're over-reacting just a little. You seem to have styled yourself as a knight in shining armour for her, and I admit she makes a rather sweet damsel in distress, but——'

'*Knight in*—— Now you're being *completely* ridiculous! Honestly, Faye, will you just. . .?'

And at that point his voice faded as Belinda got herself safely into the passage and out of earshot at last. If her cheeks had been hot when he arrived, they were on fire now. Faye Hamilton and her brother both thought of her as a sweet little thing who needed protection, did they? Well, she shouldn't be surprised, because it was quite an accurate assessment. Not an unkind one, either. Clearly both meant well, but their concern only called attention to the gulf between their world, their experience, and her own.

That the gulf existed was something she had known all along, so what she had overheard and the realisation it brought with it shouldn't be causing tears to prick behind her eyes as she opened the cupboard in the study that adjoined Faye and Bill's bedroom, and got out the testing kit she had come for. So why *were* there tears?

'I've just gone all stupidly emotional because he touched me again!' she whispered to herself. 'Well, I *won't*, and that's all there is to it!'

Taking a firm stand against her own silliness definitely helped, and she was able to return to the veranda holding the kit in steady hands and wearing a cheerful smile.

'I'll do it,' said Faye, reaching her hands out for the kit. 'Mrs Porter's going to bring you a tomato juice.'

'Oh, thanks,' said Belinda, knowing that this was an apology from Faye, as well as a mothering gesture to placate her brother's anger.

The artist calmly took a small mechanical device and positioned it against the side of her finger which wore a glittering pair of rings in emerald and diamond. She clicked it and took it away to reveal the red drop of blood that the tiny lancet's pin prick had produced. Wiping away the first drop, which might be contaminated by perspiration, she waited until a second drop formed, then pressed her finger on to the chemically treated reagent strip. Then she handed it to her brother.

'Wash it off and put it in the meter for me, would you, Tom? I want to rest my eyes.'

'Not having any trouble with your eyes, are you?' he asked smoothly as he rinsed off the reagent strip, but Belinda saw that his own eyes were alert beneath the veiling fringe of sooty lashes.

'No, but I'm not taking any chances. I know pregnancy creates an added risk of retinopathy, and I'm seeing my ophthalmologist next week, but that's not enough. If I went blind and couldn't paint. . .'

'You're *not* going to go blind, Faye!' he told her firmly.

'No, I'm *not*! And resting my eyes doesn't have much to do with it, I'm sure, but I'm darn well going to rest them anyway.'

'It certainly doesn't hurt,' her brother agreed. 'And your blood sugar is sixty-two.'

'Pretty normal for pre-lunch,' said Faye. 'but I'd better eat soon.'

'What's on the menu?' asked Tom.

'Cold chicken, hot bread rolls, lots of salads.'

'Tempting!'

'Stay!' Faye invited.

'I can't.' He glanced at Belinda as he spoke and she turned quickly to the glucose monitoring kit to put it away. Had her face betrayed disappointment? 'But I'll see you tonight.'

Out of the corner of her eye, Belinda saw that his glance took in both of them, but she said nothing. Faye had said last night that she would be welcome at the informal gathering, but, 'I'm planning to visit my family,' Belinda had explained truthfully, after politely declining the invitation.

The day went by uneventfully after Tom had left— lunch, another blood glucose test, Faye's nap, and more painting, punctuated by snacks at carefully planned intervals. At five o'clock, after giving Faye a foot massage to stimulate circulation, Belinda was free for the evening, and the unfinished painting was put away in Faye's studio at the back of the house to dry over the weekend.

'It doesn't look like much yet,' Belinda reported to her father two hours later. 'I thought she'd do it bit by bit in detail, but she doesn't. She does washes of background colour over the whole canvas, then builds the shapes and colours up gradually. I'm still just a blur.'

'You'll have to get a photo of it when it's finished,' Ian Jones said as he finished the meal of fish, salad and chips that Belinda had prepared as soon as she arrived. 'No one in our family has ever had their portrait painted before.'

'Oh, it's not really a portrait,' Belinda explained, feeling on very shaky ground. 'It's—I think it's supposed to be part of a series. It's *saying* something—but I have to admit I don't know what!'

Her father chuckled heartily at this admission, his work-hardened shoulders shaking comfortably. 'It's a pity the boys aren't here,' he said a minute later.

'I'll make the rest of the fish into a kedgeree,' Belinda told him.

'I don't mean that, love. It would have been nice for us to be all together, that's all. . .but they're growing up now. They've got other. . .'

'Fish to fry,' she joined with him, and rolled her eyes, having seen the awful pun—typical of Dad— coming just in the nick of time. 'Yes, I suppose they have, these days.'

They had a cup of tea, then chatted for a while longer while Belinda made the kedgeree and Mr Jones washed the dishes, then the latter said with a grimace, 'I've got to go now too, love. There's paperwork I have to get done at the store before tomorrow.'

'And do you think the boys'll be back soon?' she asked.

He shook his head. 'Andrew's gone to a six o'clock movie with some mates, then they'll grab hamburgers somewhere, and the twins are staying the night at a friend's.'

There was little reason to stay on in an empty house, Belinda decided as she covered and refrigerated the kedgeree after her father had left. There was no cleaning or tidying to be done. The white enamel of the stove-top gleamed, and the old family dog's food and water bowl in the laundry was freshly scrubbed and filled. Running her finger suspiciously along the top of the fridge, she found it to be commendably dust-free.

As well, the rest of the house was as near to immaculate as a house could be when it contained three teenage boys and a busy man. Mrs Jelbart must be working out well as a housekeeper, and from a couple of things her father had said, Belinda gathered that she seemed to care about the Jones boys in a more personal way too. Her father was obviously pleased about that. His face had softened noticebly when he talked about Jean's knack of. . .

'He's falling in love with her,' Belinda whispered to the empty kitchen. The realisation, which came to her and the unmistakable clarity of truth, was quite a shock.

'I want him to be happy. . . She seems nice. . . Oh, lord, I hope she feels the same way about him! But it's so sudden. . .and I don't feel as if I'm needed here any more. That's why this all feels so funny—I'm used to them all *needing* me.'

The thoughts tumbled confusedly together as she drove back to the Hamiltons' in the small car they had put at her disposal. She went to Indooroophilly because she lived there now, and in an evening that had turned rather sad and sour she didn't know what else to do. By the time she arrived, still wrestling with this dramatic rearrangement of the stars in the family constellation, she had the beginnings of a bad headache, and it was only as she turned into the drive and saw the lights and heard voices and music spilling from the house that she thought about the party that was still, clearly, very much in progress.

Parking the car in the small space beneath the house that had been set aside for it, Belinda skimmed silently up the back stairs. If she could only gain her room unnoticed, she would be able to sit quietly in the rocking chair with a book and——

But when she took a necessary short cut through the kitchen, she wasn't at all surprised to find that the figure filling the doorway with a tray of drinks balanced in his hands was Tom.

CHAPTER FIVE

'So YOU'RE going to lend your presence to this occasion after all?' Tom said at once, typically light and teasing.

'Oh!' she blurted. 'No, I. . .was just going to my room.'

'Don't be ridiculous! Come and join in.'

'I'd rather——' she began.

'Belinda!' Suddenly he was close to her, the drinks tray slid expertly on to a counter-top, and she could almost feel the warmth that emanated from his skin. 'If this is because you feel you're only being asked out of politeness. . . You *must* learn to have a little more confidence in your. . .' he hesitated, his firmly-moulded lips slightly parted as he searched for a word '. . .desirability.'

Belinda grew hot at once. He wasn't saying he thought her desirable, was he? No, he wasn't. 'As a party guest,' he added quickly, as if he had guessed her timid and disbelieving interpretation of the word. A hand came up to rumple the short hair at the back of his head, a gesture that betrayed his momentary awkwardness.

'But I have a headache,' she blurted bluntly and desperately, to cover her embarrassment.

'Well, I prescribe aspirin,' he countered. 'In fact, I know Mrs Porter keeps some right here.'

He turned to a small cabinet mounted high on the kitchen wall, and in a moment had presented her with a glass of water and two white capsules that she

69

swallowed obediently and not without relief. Her head really was starting to pound.

'Now,' he said coaxingly, 'how about slipping into something a little more festive?'

They both glanced down at her cotton jersey skirt and matching aqua-blue blouse, and Belinda saw, as he must have seen, that the outfit was looking a little tired at this stage in the day.

'By the time you've done that,' he pointed out, 'your headache will be gone.'

He had begun to coax her in the direction of her room now, the drinks tray left forgotten on the counter-top, and she went along helplessly, carried by the tide of his will and of her own incurable need to be with him.

'Have a quick shower too,' he suggested when they reached the door of her room. 'That headache has tightened you up all over—or perhaps it was the tightness that gave you the headache in the first place.' He studied her with narrowed eyes, then brushed a cool palm across her forehead to smooth the frown imprinted there. 'See you in a little while.'

'Mm-hm,' Belinda nodded tremulously, fighting her overpowering desire to surrender herself even further to his gentle ministrations. She slipped into her room and closed the door of the bathroom behind her, drawing a breath of relief at being alone. She *did* need a shower to wash away the tension from a day that had been too full of emotion. Tingling needles of hot water and a rich lather of rose-scented soap began to work magic, and the aspirin started to take effect too.

Swathed in a thick towel, she emerged several min-utes later from the bathroom, thinking that if she donned jeans and a pullover against the cooling night she could slip down into the garden and breathe some fresh air by the river. Surely Tom would have rejoined the other guests and forgotten all about her by now?

But he hadn't. She saw him as soon as she started across the room towards the antique chest of drawers where her casual clothes were kept. That silhouette leaning over the railing of the darkened veranda just beyond her window was definitely his. He had waited for her. Had he guessed she would try to slip away? And if she *did* slip away, why did it matter to him?

I must tell him, she thought feverishly. I must tell him to *stop*! I'm *not* a child, I don't need all this protection and concern!

Quickly she put on lacy underwear and pulled her best dress from the wardrobe, a cocktail-length skirt of full, flame-coloured taffeta topped by a portrait-necked bodice of black velvet. It was a bridesmaid's dress, left over from her cousin's wedding in Charters Towers last year, and she had not worn it since, but the brief glimpse she had had of the other female guests had told her that her more casual outfits would not do tonight amongst the Hamiltons' sophisticated entourage.

Fluffing her hair in a fine halo around her head with brisk brush strokes, and sketching in warm-toned eye-shadow, mascara and lipstick, Belinda was soon ready to slip into matt black court shoes and go out to the veranda.

'You didn't need to wait,' she told Tom calmly.

He turned, and she saw the approval in his face.

'But I wanted to wait,' he said. 'And it was well worth it.'

His sweeping yet detailed glance told her he was thoroughly accustomed to the sight of a well-dressed woman, and she knew that in spite of his compliment he would recognise this dress as the countrified imitation of city fashions that it was. She twitched the rustling rayon taffeta skirt apologetically. 'I'm sure Faye's friends. . .' She trailed off.

He nodded. 'Yes, straight out of *Vogue*, most of them. But that dress is lovely. It suits you. It doesn't matter that it's not real silk.'

There was a moment of silence as their gazes locked, and his last sentence seemed to hang in the air, as if it had a meaning beyond the surface value of the words.

'Ready to go?' he asked at last, but she hesitated and ducked her head, and he stepped towards her. 'Hey!' It was very gentle. 'Am I really forcing you into this?'

'No, you're not forcing me. I should——'

'No "should" about it. Do you want——? Oh, damn! Never mind! What *I* want is. . .'

She hadn't expected his kiss at all, and when his warm lips closed over her tight, trembling mouth she gasped, stiffened, felt her defences crashing, and found a tremulous yet passionate response all in a matter of seconds. Her lips parted uncertainly and she tasted the sweet caress of his mouth like a child tasting fizzy sherbet for the first time.

It was delightful, overwhelming, terrifying, inexpressibly wonderful. She wanted to explore this, him, the entire sensation of it, for hours. She wanted to run her fingers through his hair, wanted to nuzzle her nose and chin into his neck, wanted to know the texture of his cheek and jaw, wanted to kiss him so that her lips never forgot the shape of his. Then she found she was doing all this already, and a sigh of utter contentment shivered through her.

She had never imagined that a kiss could feel like this, that a man's arms could enclose and shield her so thoroughly against any other awareness, that her body would respond so passionately and so completely from the roots of her hair to the backs of her knees. She was tingling all over, on fire, melting. . .

Seconds later she was suddenly aware that he had drawn gently away, and her eyes flew open in shock as she felt his firm hand untangling her fingers from his hair. Both her hands were imprisoned in his now, and he was staring down at them.

'Oh, lord!' She heard the groaned exclamation of regret. 'I don't believe this!'

'What is it? What's wrong? Did I. . .? Didn't I. . .?' She couldn't go on.

'You've never been kissed before.' It was an accusation, and he spoke with confidence and authority.

'No,' she admitted.

How had he known? Had she. . .done it wrong? She wasn't surprised at his amazement over the fact. To have remained unkissed at twenty-two in this day and age must be a rarity—she was worldly enough to know that, at least. But his apparent disgust—was that it, was that what he felt?—shocked and appalled her.

'Never been kissed! Oh, lord!' he groaned again, and suddenly Belinda's spirit stirred into life.

She drew away and straightened herself. 'I'm not a leper, you know!'

'What?' he said absently, relaxing the tight grip on her hands at last and looking up sharply.

'I said I'm not a leper. Virginity isn't catching.' Deliberately, she made her tone harsh. He studied her . . .was it pityingly? She gave up any attempt to read him now.

'Belinda,' he said on a long sigh, 'go into the party, would you? There's a good girl. I—I must have had too much to drink. I need some air.'

'Of course. Are you all right? I can get you a cup of——'

'Just go, love,' he said, firmly.

'All right.'

And she went, her heart thudding in her chest with slow, painful beats and her mind a confused whirl. Too much to drink? His lips hadn't tasted of alcohol at all. *She* on the other hand, thought that a drink, a *strong* drink, might be exactly what she needed. She hadn't had one since. . .last Christmas, probably, but it was what people often did in films and books when their feelings were in turmoil.

She thought about how people kissed in films and books as well, trying to understand what she had done wrong, but it was no use. Her response to him had been totally instinctive, nothing to do with anything she had read or seen. She didn't know why her lack of experience had thrown him so utterly, and she thought now that perhaps she didn't *want* to know.

Obviously their kiss had been a mistake and a fiasco from the start, and her own wariness about her naïve feelings for him had rung warning bells in her mind since his first mention of a 'private nursing job'. If she had listened to those warning bells more carefully. . . Except that that kiss and her response to it had taken her so much by surprise that, even in hindsight, she did not see how she could have forestalled it.

The party had quietened in the half-hour since Belinda had turned into the driveway, but music, laughter and conversation still flowed over her with a welcome wave of sound that drowned the thudding pulse in her ears and the silent clamour of her thoughts. Bill Hamilton smiled across the room at her and pointed at a side table where drinks and appetising titbits were laid out.

Helping herself to what looked like a gin and tonic— and was a very strong one, she found when she tasted it—as well as a tiny chicken and mushroom vol-au-vent, she was about to make a beeline for an unoccupied chair in the corner when a stranger spoke beside her.

'We haven't met, have we?' he smiled.

'No, we haven't,' acknowledged Belinda. 'I'm Mrs Hamilton's nurse, Belinda Jones.'

'Faye's nurse? Well, you're certainly not in uniform tonight!'

'No.'

'Bill mentioned that you'd started work here—I'm an associate of his, by the way, Greg Carey—but he didn't mention how lovely you were.'

'Oh! No, I'm sure he didn't.' It came out more drily than she had intended, and black-haired Greg Carey laughed, interpreting her tone as one of irony.

'You're right, Bill's not the sort of man to include information like that in casual conversation. He's a boringly faithful husband, eyes only for one woman, etcetera. All the same, you *are* lovely, with a gorgeous smile which I bet brightens Faye's day no end.'

'Thank you,' smiled Belinda.

'And now, if you'll excuse me. . .' He picked up a gin and tonic from the same tray where Belinda had found hers, sipped it and made a face. 'Mm! Strong!' Then he crossed the room to collar a departing guest for some last words and they went out of the front door together.

Alone again, Belinda returned to her original plan and successfully reached the chair in the corner of the room, from which she could quietly observe the other guests without too much fear of attracting attention. There were only about seven people left now out of the dozen or so who had been gathered here earlier. It was, as Tom had said it would be, a fairly small affair.

Faye lay on an Oriental couch amid a pile of silk brocade cushions and was happy to have the party guests come to her instead of herself circling amongst them. In one hand she held an iced tonic water and on a small table beside her was a cocktail plate of spicy-fried chicken wings. Just how spicy-fried Belinda found out very soon as a smiling older woman passed around the dish of hot, plump morsels.

She had been eating mechanically until now—the vol-au-vent, some olives, a sliver of cheese—trying unsuccessfully to drown the sensation of Tom's kiss that she could still taste and feel so strongly on her lips, but, as soon as she bit into the juicy chicken wing with its sizzling red coating of spiced crumbs, her mouth began to burn with a very different feeling.

Unused to spicy food, she took a long mouthful of the gin and tonic, which she could now no longer even taste, then very deliberately she finished the chicken wing and ate another one. This burning sensation was infinitely preferable, at the moment, to the imprint of Tom Russell's lips.

'Where's Tom?' she heard a lovely brunette ask Faye. 'He seems to have completely disappeared.'

'Don't worry,' said Greg Carey, who had returned from ushering out his fellow guest. 'I caught sight of him in the garden a moment ago—at least, I'm pretty sure that brooding silhouette was his, looming in the shrubbery—and he wasn't seducing anyone as far as I could see.'

'Don't be more stupid than you can help, Greg!' the brunette hissed darkly.

'Sorry, Marise,' the architect grinned unrepentantly.

He seemed to regard the exchange purely as a joke, but Marise continued to glower beneath her perfectly drawn black brows, and Faye too looked irritated by

Greg's words. She put down her drink and shifted
restlessly against her patchwork backdrop of glowing
cushions, and her face, above an Oriental-cut trouser-
suit in black silk, looked suddenly pale. Greg was still
laughing—forcedly, it seemed to Belinda—at a joke
that no one else had shared, then abruptly he grabbed
his drink from the table beside Faye and crossed the
room again.

Only it wasn't *his* drink he had picked up, Belinda
realised immediately; it was Faye's.

The pregnant woman, having just made a face at the
taste of the spicy chicken wings, just as Belinda had
done, was about to take a sip of Greg's very strong gin
and tonic.

It's all right, thought Belinda, she'll know straight
away from the taste.

But no, she wouldn't. Not with the spicy heat from
the chicken wings still in her mouth.

'Faye. . . Mrs Hamilton!' Breathlessly, Belinda
arrived at the artist's side, her cheeks burning at having
to intrude on a conversation that was just getting
established again after Greg's tactless attempt at
humour.

'What is it, Belinda?' Faye turned to her on a
suppressed sigh. She definitely looked tired now.

'That's not your drink.'

'I beg your pardon?'

'That's not your drink, it's Greg's. It's gin and tonic.
He's taken yours by mistake. Sorry to. . .but I was
watching. I saw it.'

'Really? Oh, dear! See what a jewel of a nurse I
have, Marise?' Faye responded lightly. 'Keeping a
pregnant woman away from the demon drink. Well,
that tonic water was too sweet and fizzy anyway. I'd
like some plain tapwater with a little ice, actually.'

Belinda took a step towards the kitchen, but the older woman who had passed out the chicken wings offered quickly, 'I'll get it, Faye.'

Meanwhile, Faye mouthed a discreet, 'Thanks!' to Belinda, and the latter guessed that Marise was not close enough to the Hamiltons to know of Faye's diabetic condition. Drinking alcohol was unwise for any pregnant woman, but in Faye's case, the effect of the substance on her blood-sugar levels was a more crucial factor.

'Is that really part of your job, Belinda?' Marise questioned lazily. 'I knew Faye had some complications and needed a nurse—Tom mentioned it the other day—but I had no idea you were a sort of watchdog as well. Medical matters are a complete mystery to me, frankly.'

'No, it's not part of my job,' Belinda responded steadily. 'I just happened to notice it, that's all.'

'Oh. Well, that was lucky, wasn't it?' Marise said dismissively, not really looking at Belinda as she spoke.

She's waiting for Tom to come in, the young nurse realised. She's involved with him. . .or she wants to be . . .and that's why she was so angry with Greg Carey.

The realisation made her want to study the other woman closely, and, covertly, she was able to do so, as Marise and Faye were soon involved in a discussion of the modern Japanese sculpture exhibition which had recently opened at the art gallery.

The brunette was strikingly attractive in a way that was dramatically enhanced by make-up and clothes. Her hair was glossy, perfectly straight and almost black, and it hung thickly around her perfectly-shaped head in a faultless bob that must have been done at Brisbane's most exclusive hair salon. She had black eyes, black brows and a mouth that was a bold slash of dark red against the pale—almost white—matt of her make-up.

Her tightly tailored strapless dress matched her lips exactly, as did the shoes that even Belinda recognised as highest quality Italian leather, the kind of leather with a fine grain that was almost like satin to the touch. She had a low, musical voice that owed its perfect diction to an expensive private education, and her conversation left Belinda way out of her depth.

'Tom and I saw it the other day,' she was saying. 'And I loved it. Not all the artists. One of them would be more at home doing scaffolding on a building site, in my opinion. But the others! The texture of the wood! The drama of the ideas—so simple yet so strong. Incredibly tactile and such a sense of form. You *must* see it! Or at least. . . Are you really totally confined to bed, Faye? Isn't Tom being over-protective?'

Her softened tone said she thought that this was very sweet of him, if a little unnecessary. . .and suddenly Tom himself was standing behind her and draping a light hand around her bare shoulders. Belinda saw the gesture, winced inwardly as the image stabbed at her feelings, and despised herself for wasting her emotions in this way. Of course Dr Russell would be involved with a woman like Marise. A *woman*, not a silly naïve girl like herself. It was what she had known all along. Why should it have the power to hurt her like this?

'Did I hear my name being taken in vain?' he said lightly, his blue gaze flicking quickly to Belinda's face and away again.

'I'm questioning your medical judgement,' said Marise with a mischievous, provocative arch of her brows.

'Are you?' he said absently, and Belinda could see at once that Marise was disappointed that he hadn't played along. 'Speaking of medical matters, I need to see Belinda for a moment, if you'll excuse us.'

Adroitly he slipped past Marise and drew Belinda away from the group with a hand placed lightly in the small of her back. For a moment she felt his warm breath on her half-bared shoulder, and caught a waft of the very dry, utterly masculine scent of his after-shave. His hand in her back was steady, not caressing but insistently guiding.

She didn't want to follow him. He was going to say something about their kiss and his reaction to it, and she didn't think she wanted to hear it. But still less did she want to make a scene or create any kind of curiosity amongst the people she had just left, so she allowed him to lead her from the room, saying, 'Yes, we needed to discuss those—er—charts, didn't we, Dr Russell?' in case anyone was still listening.

'Let's go into the garden,' he said tersely, and a few moments later they were gliding along the path that wound down to the river's edge, their way lit by a bright moon that stretched a blue path towards them across the water.

As they went, Belinda's thoughts were hard at work. It was a relief that he did not try to speak, and when they came out at the landscaped clearing with its wooden bench seat overlooking the water she had readied herself to speak first. Facing him, she wasted no time, the words pouring forth just as he drew a reluctant breath before speech.

'I know what you want to say,' she began, 'and it's all right. You don't have to say it. At least, I understand. It's all right.'

He was looking at her, surprised and wary, the olive-toned colours of his subtly pattered shirt and plain pants bleached by the moonlight so that they looked like grey and silver.

'What do you think I want to say?' he asked softly.

'Oh, it's obvious, isn't it? That kiss was a mistake. We both know it.' With an effort, she slowed her words to a more reasonable, measured pace. 'I understand . . .that it was a strong impulse at the time. I. . . I felt it too. Then, when you found out how. . .inexperienced I was——'

'Don't make it sound like a disease, love,' he interrupted gently.

'I'm not—I said before. . . Well, I accused you of reacting as if I was a leper. That wasn't right, and I can see that now. I can see that you realised before I did that we were both being foolish. We don't belong in each other's lives. . .' she said this part *very* firmly '. . .even at the level of an *affair*.' It wasn't a word she had used very often before.

'No, we don't,' he responded evenly. 'It couldn't possibly work at all. Least of all for you.'

She ducked her head in miserable assent, then, because his agreeing with what she had said hurt her in spite of everything, she added rashly, 'You ought to be with a woman like Marise.'

'Marise?' he queried.

'Or someone like her,' Belinda stressed, not wanting him to guess that she had noticed the brunette's special interest in him. Whatever footing the two of them were on, it was none of her business. She added firmly, 'Someone far more sophisticated than I'll ever be.'

'Really?' he murmured, on an odd note that she could not pinpoint. 'Perhaps. That's what I've always thought in the past. Lately I'd started to wonder. . . But perhaps you're right.'

There was a silence, broken only by the faint lapping

of the water. Belinda studied Tom covertly and read relief in his face, along with other emotions that she could not pinpoint. Then he took a steady pace backwards and looked down at her. 'And what about you? Some time soon the right person *is* going to want to kiss those tender lips of yours, love. Have you thought about what sort of person you want it to be?'

'I. . . No, how could I?' she asked, startled at this thought. 'Doesn't love just happen? It's not like shopping, where you have a list of——'

His bark of laughter interrupted her. 'What an idea! But you know perhaps it *is* like shopping. Isn't that what you've just been telling me? That on *my* list of desired qualities, the word "sophisticated" has to appear?'

'Don't confuse me!' she muttered, staring down at her plain fingernails, prettily almond-shaped but unmanicured and unvarnished.

'All right. But I want you to tell me—seriously!— what sort of person you think you'll want to love.'

'Hm. . . ' She looked up at him again. 'Do I have to answer?'

'Of course not. But let me give you some advice— big brotherly advice.'

'Well, I only have little brothers. This'll be a new experience,' she murmured, feeling slightly hypnotised by the moonlight, by their solitude, by his cool, sincere voice.

'Make sure it's someone who really deserves you,' Tom told her.

'Deserves me?' she queried.

'You're pretty incredible, Belinda,' he told her.

'Am I? Why?'

'I don't know! I'll have to study you more extensively and let you know.'

She laughed, a response that pleased him, then he stepped towards her and took both her hands in his, gazing steadily down at her, serious once more. 'You *are* right in what you said, and perhaps it's a good thing that all this has happened, to clear the air. Can we be friends now, with no awkwardness and no regrets?'

'I'd like that,' she agreed.

To her surprise, she felt her spirits lift on the faint, cool breeze that was coming up the river from the sea. The exchange between them had been painful, but there was something so honest and open about it that she felt freed for the first time in months from her painful awareness of him as a man. As he grinned and pulled her towards him, kissing her in a gentle, careful, comradely fashion on the forehead to seal their agreement, she knew that her crush on Dr Tom Russell was over, and something else—something better and more real, she hoped—had taken its place.

CHAPTER SIX

'I'VE gained another four hundred grammes this week,' Faye told Belinda as she settled back into the semi-reclined passenger-seat of the Saab, while Belinda herself was at the wheel.

'What did Dr Greene have to say about that?' the nurse enquired.

'He wasn't worried. I'm getting into the peak period for weight gain now. I've seventeen weeks and my total gain is seven pounds, which is on target.'

'And he did do the alpha-fetoprotein screening this week?'

'Yes, and he's going to rush it through the lab as soon as possible, he says. He's talking about amniocentesis as well, which should be done next week if its's going to be done at all.'

Faye made a face and slumped back in the passenger-seat. The weekly trip to Dr Greene was her one outing, and Belinda always drove, so that Faye could lie back comfortably. Understandably, she fretted at this circumscribed lifestyle, but another episode of somewhat more serious bleeding two weeks ago had convinced everyone that the programme of rest and professional care was not an overcautious one.

'Have you and Bill discussed the amniocentesis question?' Belinda queried carefully.

Faye laughed. 'From day one! I was adamant then that I wouldn't have it, but the idea of actually getting this far with a baby—well, I didn't want to jinx it by even thinking too much about it. Now it's actually upon us and a decision has to be made. . .'

'I wish I could help,' Belinda said slowly, 'but I can't. Dr Greene must have given you all the facts.'

'Yes, about how many different birth defects the procedure can pick up. . . Frankly, if I weren't in such a high-risk position, I'd want someone a little more *cosy* as my obstetrician, but Owen is the best for someone like me and at times he can be a dear, so I shouldn't complain. . . And he told me about the increased risk of late miscarriage with amniocentesis as well.'

'It's about one per cent, isn't it?' asked Belinda, keeping a careful eye on the road as she drove. Faye had a late afternoon appointment today, and the evening traffic was beginning. She was used to driving the luxurious Saab by this time, although at first the responsibility had unnerved her considerably.

'I believe so,' Faye answered. 'One in a hundred. It doesn't sound like much, but if someone told you those were your odds of winning the lottery, you'd buy a ticket, wouldn't you?'

'Yes, I suppose I would,' Belinda agreed.

'Well, this particular lottery is one I *don't* want to win!'

Faye said nothing more about it, but when they got home she announced that she would take her blood-sugar level and evening insulin dose in her room and then lie down on her bed until dinner. This was unusual, as she generally preferred the lounging chair on the veranda, 'so that I don't feel completely bedridden,' and Belinda hoped she was not going to lie there and brood about the issue of the amniocentesis.

'Remember your injection site for this evening?' she queried gently.

'No, but I'll look it up on the chart. Site five, I think, on the left thigh.'

The clipped, breezy tone was one that Belinda knew by this time, and it meant, I want to be left to myself for the time being, thank you. Respecting this wish, she let her patient go to her room alone.

Sitting on the veranda herself a short while later as she worked on a lacy white shawl she was secretly knitting for the baby, Belinda murmured aloud, 'I hope Tom comes today. Perhaps he's the person to talk to her.'

His name flowed off her tongue without effort or pain. It was over six weeks since she had come to work here, and six weeks to the day since his kiss and their painfully honest talk down by the river beneath the moonlight. In that six weeks they had become friends, and it was a very satisfying feeling.

He often dropped in at this time of day, and frequently stayed for a drink on the veranda and an inspection of Faye's work in the air-conditioned studio at the back of the house that would be used more and more as the hot summer approached. Sometimes he was even prevailed upon to stay for dinner, which was usually a casual meal with everyone grouped around Faye and the wheeled tray that was placed in front of her on the padded lounge seat where she spent so much of her time.

But today's Friday. I suppose he'll be going out, she realised, and acknowledged to herself that she was a little disappointed. . .for Faye's sake, of course.

Tom talked to Belinda very frankly about the women in his life—yes, it was plural—these days. There was dark-haired Marise, red-headed Paula and blonde Wendy, all involved in the arts in some way, as well as a rather serious and intense kidney specialist from the hospital, Dr Terri Myers, who was separated from her husband and was two or three years older than Tom himself. If any of these women were seriously important to him, she couldn't tell from his attitude, so she was able to listen quite happily when he spoke about a play he had seen with Paula, or repeated an anecdote of Wendy's about her job as a television production assistant.

Fifteen minutes passed and no car turned into the shaded driveway. He's *not* coming, she decided. Oh, well. Faye still has a few more days to consider the amniocentesis.

It was only a few seconds later, just as she was finishing an easy row of plain knitting, that she heard the tinkle of Faye's bell, a clamorous, urgent sound that cut across the dreamy mood of the October afternoon. After quickly rolling the half-completed shawl into a loose parcel anchored with its plastic needles, Belinda hurried to answer the bell, not particularly alarmed. Faye often rang for her, and the jangling, impatient note of the bell was merely characteristic of Faye's vibrant, dramatic personality. A polite little tinkle, now *that* would be something to cause concern!

'Is anything wrong, Faye?' She entered the room after a gentle knock, and saw that Faye was lying on her back in the large, luxurious bed, her shoulders raised on pillows and her fingers massaging her abdomen tentatively.

'I don't know,' the artist confessed. 'I'm having some funny pains.'

'Bad ones?'

'No, not *bad*.' Faye frowned. 'In fact, "pains" is too strong. Aches—twinges, I suppose.'

'So you don't think you're in labour?' Belinda pressed, very relieved.

'Oh, heavens, no! I'm probably blowing it way out of proportion, but everything upsets me these days. That blood sugar was higher than it usually is. . .' Faye sniffed and gulped as threatened tears became a reality.

'Not significantly?'

'No, but then I've been thinking about the amniocentesis. It's such a *hugely* important decision, and. . . look at me. I'm in floods of tears over nothing! Get me my tissues, love. The box in the bathroom is empty, you'll have to go out to the veranda.'

'I'll only be a moment. . .and maybe we'll do an extra blood-sugar reading in a little while to make sure being upset isn't making it go wonky.'

Belinda hurried back to the veranda and found the tissues, wondering if she was being overcautious about the blood sugar. But she had started to notice that Faye's level of stress or unhappiness seemed to have an unusually dramatic effect on her blood glucose. Perhaps it was her artistic temperament—it was impossible to know for certain. But it meant that an important part of Belinda's work was to be on the alert for this kind of upset and do everything she could to minimise its effect.

She didn't know what Faye's pain could be. Many pregnant women felt discomfort as their ligaments and muscles began to stretch to accommodate their growing uterus and the life it contained. On the other hand, it could be a gastric upset. Or it could simply be activity in the digestive tract.

But what was that patch of dark red she glimpsed in the driveway, through the shading trees?

'Tom!' The latticework door at the edge of the veranda opened at that moment and she hurried towards him, not troubling to disguise her pleasure at his arrival.

'Hi!' He touched her shoulder in a light, friendly caress and grinned down at her, seeming pleased too.

'I'm so glad you've come!' she told him.

'I'm flattered.'

'Silly! No, it's Faye.'

'Nothing wrong?' A frown wiped away the smile instantly, and alertness replaced relaxed cheerfulness.

He was dressed in work clothes—tailored dark grey trousers and a cream shirt—but the latter was open at the neck and he wore no tie, suggesting that he had been ready for a relaxing Friday evening drink. Belinda hoped he would get one.

'Well, she's complaining of twinges in her abdomen,' she told him. 'But I don't think that's the real problem.'

'No?'

'It's this whole issue of the amniocentesis.'

'Ah, yes! Dr Greene did the alpha-fetoprotein screening today, didn't he?'

'Yes, and he told her she should have the amnio in the next week if she's going to have it at all. And he wants her to have it, particularly if there's any departure from normal in the a.fp levels. She was lying there worrying about that when she started to feel these twinges.'

'Probably the ligaments starting to stretch.'

'Yes, that's what I thought. She got a bit upset.' Belinda held up the box of tissues. 'I thought I'd take another blood glucose reading just in case.'

'Let's go and see what we can do.' Tom touched her shoulder again.

'If you could talk to her about the amnio. . .'

He nodded briefly, then turned to enter the house with Belinda following closely in the wake of his capable stride and feeling very thankful that he had arrived.

'Look who's here!' she said unnecessarily as she entered Faye's bedroom behind him.

Her bright tone brought a reluctant smile to Faye's lips, then she dabbed her swollen eyes with the tissues Belinda gave her and tried to struggle to a sitting position.

'Lie down, Faye,' said Tom. 'Let's see about these pains. There's no nausea, is there? It's not something you ate?'

'No, and they've stopped now. I'm over-reacting— hormones again.'

'Let's have a check anyway.' He began to palpate her abdomen carefully, pressing with firm, expert fingers. 'Everything feels fine—nice and hard and getting bigger every day. Nothing untoward at your check-up this morning?'

'No.'

'And no bleeding since that episode two weeks ago?'

Faye shook her head.

'Then I think it *is* your ligaments stretching. You probably felt it today because you were up and about at the doctor's. Belinda says he wants you to make a decision about the amnio. . .'

It was the moment when Belinda felt she should leave. 'I'll be on the veranda, Tom,' she murmured, and he and his sister both nodded.

They emerged together half an hour later, just as Bill's car pulled into the driveway. Faye looked much happier, although Tom was saying, 'It has to be your decision—yours and Bill's. You can play it by the odds, by intuition, or by what you feel is morally right, but you and Bill are the ones who have to live with the result. Just remember that whatever you decide the worst case scenario is very unlikely to happen.'

'Let's not talk about it any more now, Tom.'

'No. Wait until you and Bill have some time to yourselves. Is this the fruit of your labours for the week?'

To change the subject he turned to an easel in the most sheltered corner of the veranda, and the painting propped on it that had not yet been put away in Faye's studio.

'Yes,' said Faye. 'I finished it this morning. Turn it around so I can have another look at it. I liked it six hours ago, but will I still?'

'You know you never do, you temperamental creature,' Tom pointed out. 'The euphoria of completion seems to last you about ten minutes.'

He turned the picture so that Faye could see it, as well as Belinda and Bill, who had just arrived, briefcase in hand and shirt collar rather tired-looking after his long day. Belinda, as usual, flushed at the sight of the boldly executed canvas. Being an artist's model was turning out to be somewhat more traumatic than she had anticipated.

For one thing, the figure in each painting never looked very much like herself. In Faye's first painting, she had turned out so wraithlike and ethereal that she had secretly weighed herself on Faye's bathroom scales to make sure she still came in at fifty-three kilograms. In the second painting, every irregularity in her figure had been emphasised so that the girl stretching outwards from a balcony to pick a ripe, hanging fruit appeared as misshapen as a fairy-tale goblin.

This picture, the third in Faye's series, focused more fully on her face and the likeness of features and form was very good, but it showed her with such a yearning, wistful expression that everyone who saw it and knew her would think her life had been one long secret sorrow.

'What do you think, Belinda?' Tom asked, with a touch of impatience, then added in an aside to Faye and Bill, 'See, she's so impressed she hasn't even heard me!'

'Oh!' She started guiltily, and flushed even more deeply. Everyone seemed to be waiting for her reaction, and she saw that Tom, in particular, was observing her narrowly. Quickly she manufactured enthusiasm. 'It's lovely! I mean, obviously it is. The colours of the shadows—I'd never thought how rich they are. If I'd been painting shadows they'd have been blue or grey, but real shadows aren't nearly so simple!'

There, would that do? Evidently not. 'But what does it *say* to you, love?' Faye demanded cajolingly. 'I can never get you to tell me how it makes you *feel*, what it *communicates*.'

'Er—well. . .'

'For heaven's sake, Faye—she's not an art critic!' Tom put in irritably.

'No, I know, but that's good. I like to hear the reaction of someone who has no experience of art. I get so sick of rarefied jargon. Belinda is uncorrupted by nefarious influences.'

But Tom didn't respond to his sister's words. Instead, he turned to Belinda and said matter-of-factly, 'Why don't we have dinner together tonight? In fact, why don't we have dinner together *now*? Do you have any plans?'

'Er—no, I don't.' These days she usually went to see her family on a week night when all the boys were certain to be home. 'But. . .'

'No buts. Would you like to?'

'Of course.'

'Of course? Good. I'll give you twenty minutes to get ready.'

'Oh, I can be ready in ten, but. . .' She glanced uncertainly at Faye.

'Go, love,' the painter said, and Bill gave a wink and a nod.

Accordingly, Belinda left the veranda and went to her room, deciding on the way that she would wear her new black evening trousers and the pale apricot silk camisole top she had bought to go with them. It was the first silk garment she had owned, and it had been expensive, but Faye's silk clothes always looked and felt so wonderful. . .

It didn't take her long to dress, freshen her make-up and add touches of silver jewellery on ears, neck and wrists, and it was quite a bit less than Tom's stipulated twenty minutes later when she approached the veranda again. Tom, Faye and Bill were still talking there, and as she crossed the entrance foyer that led out to the veranda on this side, she heard her own name.

'All I'm saying,' it was Tom's voice, 'is that I don't think you should pester Belinda to give you her opinion on your work. It isn't fair.'

Belinda froze. She couldn't bear to open the door and see them trying to cover their embarrassment at her entrance.

'*Why* isn't it fair?' Faye demanded.

'Because firstly she feels embarrassed at not knowing much about art, and secondly she's still struggling with the fact that you mould her like a piece of clay in every painting.'

'What on earth do you mean by that, Tom?'

'Darling, you are a little ruthless when it comes to your art, you know,' Bill put in mildly. 'I'm not sure that *I'd* care to expose myself to the distortions you wreak upon your subject's features.'

'Yes, remember William Dobell and that scandal over the Archibald Prize back in. . .the forties, was it?' put in Tom. 'I've read about it. There was a court case over whether his painting was a portrait or a caricature. I think Belinda feels——'

'All right, all right,' Faye interrupted crossly, 'I see what you mean. But she'll be back soon. Let's not discuss it any further.'

A moody silence descended between brother and sister, and after a judicious interval, Belinda painted a smile on her face and joined them, hoping her cheeks were not as flushed as they felt.

'Ready!' she said brightly, and Tom jumped to his feet at once, as if eager to get away. Scarcely giving her time to say goodbye, and giving Faye no time to admire Belinda's outfit, as the latter was wistfully hoping she might do, he whisked her down the front steps, opened the passenger door of the red sports car and bundled her inside.

'You didn't have to stand up for me just then,' she said steadily as soon as he had pulled out of the driveway.

'Stand up for——? Oh, you overheard!'

'Just at the end. I'm sorry. I. . .was too embarrassed to let Faye know, so I waited until. . .'

'Until we'd finished. Your trouble is that you get dressed too quickly! Faye would have taken at least half an hour.'

'Yes, but then she always looks so much nicer than I do,' Belinda responded guilelessly.

Tom gave her a sharp glance, then frowned at the road ahead once more. 'Nonsense!' Then, after a terse pause, 'Are you fishing for a compliment?'

'No! I——'

'Good! You look lovely tonight. I was going to tell you so, but you didn't give me a chance.'

'I wasn't fishing,' Belinda repeated, mortified. 'I just meant—Faye has such good taste. She does such clever things with make-up and jewellery. She always looks so—flamboyant.'

'But would you really like to look *flamboyant*? Really?' The word was spoken with gently teasing mimicry.

'I would, in some ways. . .' Belinda answered thoughtfully, intrigued by this idea. 'But actually, no, I don't think it would go with my personality.'

'Sensible girl! No, I don't think it would.'

He was silent after this, but Belinda went on thinking about the subject for some minutes more. It was true, she didn't want to look like a timid imitation of Faye, but at the same time the possibility of learning more about style was an attractive one. She already felt that she was learning something about art.

Faye had said that of course she was welcome to browse through the large collection of beautiful books on painting and sculpture that filled an entire wall of bookshelves in the studio, and she had begun to learn something about the Renaissance, Impressionism, and modern Australian painting. It was only a beginning, but. . .Tom's overheard words on the veranda returned to her. 'She feels embarrassed at not knowing much about art.' One day that might no longer be true. She realised that he hadn't ever responded to her first mildly scolding words as they left the Hamiltons'. But the subject had shifted, and now it was too late. . .or was it?

'As for my standing up for you,' he said now, out of the blue, 'why don't you want me to?'

'Because I'm not a child. I can stand up for myself.'

'So you're going to tell me you *like* the way Faye plays with your face and figure on her canvases?'

'Of course I don't,' Belinda answered matter-of-factly. 'I don't suppose anybody does, at first, unless the painting is an airbrushed portrait that makes them look perfect. It's the same as no one liking the sound of their voice on a tape-recorder. But I'm starting to get used to it, it's fascinating to find out about the way an artist works—and it's a darn sight better than putting up with a patient who's frustrated because she isn't getting anything done!'

He laughed. 'The lesser of two evils, eh?'

'Something like that!'

Shortly after this they pulled into a small car park beside an old restored colonial house that was overhung by leafy trees and lit inside and out with softly golden lamps against the gathering dusk. Having expected a casual Italian place, Belinda was a little perturbed to realise that this was L'Epoque, Brisbane's newest and most talked-about French restaurant, which must surely have required a booking in advance.

'I rang while you were getting ready,' Tom admitted, 'I was lucky. There'd just been a cancellation.'

She didn't ask him why he had chosen such an expensive place, although she privately resolved to have the cheapest items on the menu. After all, his impulsive invitation—made largely, she guessed, so that Faye and Bill could be alone for the evening to talk over the difficult issues of the amniocentesis—was not on a par with his dates with Marise or Paula.

But her menu, when it arrived, had no prices on it at all. She twitched the hand-written parchment pages back and forth for a moment or two looking for them, then caught his amused glance.

'I was. . .trying to decide if. . .'

'I know what you were doing,' he said, lightly accusing, and she knew he did. 'I made sure they gave you one *without* the prices.'

'Oh.'

He was still chuckling lazily, and for some reason his laugh was very infectious. Soon they were both laughing openly, and it was only when they took refuge in a close study of the menu that they were able to regain the control that the supercilious wine waiter clearly thought appropriate to his establishment.

'You know, Belinda Jones,' said Tom, after they had ordered, 'I find you vastly entertaining.'

'I don't know why,' she retorted crisply.

'Neigther do I,' he admitted candidly. 'Because you're so *fresh*, I think. One can get very sick of other people's jaded palates.'

'I'm sure Dr Myers doesn't have a jaded palate!' she exclaimed, picking her personal favourite amongst the candidates for his serious interest.

'Terri? No, she doesn't,' he admitted. 'Had you decided she was the woman for me?'

'Oh, of course not! I——'

'Well, in any case, she's still in love with Hayden— her husband—although she doesn't know it. I'm sure they'll be back together again soon. So be honest, Belinda, since we've agreed that we're friends.' Tom leaned forward, ignoring the piping hot servings of lobster *meunière* which had just been set reverently in front of them. 'Should it be Paula, or Wendy, or Marise?'

'I haven't even met Wendy,' said Belinda.

'No, but I've told you about her, haven't I?'

'I don't think it's appropriate for me to give an opinion,' Belinda replied firmly, 'even as a friend.'

And he laughed again. 'You're right, of course—as usual. So, try the lobster and tell me what you think.'

They lingered for two hours over the meal. Belinda was amazed when she noted the time on an antique clock that ticked on the mantelpiece over the elaborately restored fireplace near where they sat. What on earth had they talked about? He had teased her a little, as usual. And she had teased him back. They had shared some secrets about ambitions, dislikes, fears.

Friendship with a man was nice, she decided, never having experienced it before this. It gave her a warm, relaxed, glowing feeling inside. It made her notice things more, and feel more alive. It gave her added sensitivity to other people's feelings. And it gave her the security of knowing there was someone she could talk to, someone she could count on. Utterly different from that silly, crushy feeling she had had for Tom before, when all that had happened was that she had felt miserably self-conscious and tongue-tied in his presence.

They walked out to his car together in a contented silence, and when they got there he came round to the passenger side to hold back the low tendrils of an overhanging jasmine vine so she could slide easily into the seat.

At least, that was his original intention. But as they stood there with the white jasmine making an aura of perfume around their heads, something in the mood of the evening seemed to change.

'Belinda, if I kiss you, will it spoil things between us?' he asked in a low tone.

'I. . .I don't know.'

'May I try it and see?'

'I think so.'

He did, bending towards her, holding her chin in a

feather-light caress and touching her lips gently with his own. Her eyes drifted shut and she gave herself up to the kiss's magic, her own lips even more gentle and tentative than his. The touch of his lips against hers, so intimate, lasted only a moment, then his mouth travelled upwards to touch her nose and forehead, then went to her cheeks and her temples, each instant of pressure warm and almost. . .could it be. . . thoughtful?

Finally he drew away and looked down at her. There was no moon tonight, and his eyes were like midnight-blue pools, unreadable in the darkness.

'Do you think we're getting a little confused about the nature of our relationship?' he asked lightly.

'No,' she replied steadily. 'We're not confused. It's a friendship. It's good. And often a good thing is sealed with a kiss, isn't it?'

'Shall we seal it again, then?'

'Yes . . .'

This time there was no doubt about it. It was a thorough kiss. His arms came around her and she pressed willingly into them, lifting her chin and stretching up on her toes so that he did not have to bend so far towards her. Their noses bumped gently together and their mouths tasted and explored and caressed hungrily.

When his hands spread their warmth across the small of her back and dropped lower to hold the softness of her curved and very feminine hips, her own fingers found and explored the short silky curls at the nape of his neck and the hardness of the muscles that plaited across his broad, capable back. She began to feel the urgent rise and fall of his chest against the compact roundness of her young breasts, and knew a tingling awareness in them that threaded through her entire body in a way that was completely new to her and utterly wonderful.

Finally, as sensation attained an almost unbearable intensity and every drop of blood throbbed in her veins, he drew away.

'Sealed now?' he breathed, clearly with an effort.

'Yes.'

'Then perhaps we ought to get you back to Faye's, before either of us decides——' He broke off, took a ragged breath and didn't finish.

Trembling and overwhelmed, Belinda slid into the passenger-seat, feeling its cool leather against her hot skin like a new caress, her nerve-endings were so alive to every sensation now. They drove in silence, and when she dared to glance across at him she found an expression on his face that she could not read at all. He seemed to be deeply immersed in thought and was driving mechanically, his skill at the wheel a product of experience and finely honed reflexes, not of intense concentration.

'I'll see you in,' he said when the car's engine died on a last throaty purr in the Hamiltons' driveway.

'There's no need,' she told him.

'Well, Faye might still be up, and I'd like to see how she is.'

'Oh, of course, in that case. . .'

This time he didn't open the door for her, and she had difficulty keeping up as he took the front stairs two at a time. Ahead of her, Belinda heard the front door open, then Faye's voice as she greeted her brother.

'You shouldn't be up,' Tom growled ominously, but Faye laughed.

'Just this once, surely! I feel so happy, I wanted to tell you—and you, Belinda. The baby's moving! It's been happening for a few days, but I've only just realised what it is. . . Like an eyelid twitching, a tiny, tiny fluttering feeling, and tonight it's got so strong its unmistakable.'

'Faye!' He enclosed her in a bear-hug that showed the difference in size between them. For all her vitality, Faye was only five feet four inches tall, while Tom was a good ten inches taller.

Belinda stood back, smiling and pressing her hands together with pleasure. You got very involved with a patient in a situation like this. Too involved, perhaps, if you weren't careful. She felt as happy about the news as she would have done if the baby had been a future niece or nephew.

Tom released his sister and coaxed her back inside. 'Don't take any risks now, though, love. I know you're chafing at the bit, but we don't want to risk a third bleed from that low-lying placenta.'

'No, all right,' she agreed soberly. 'See, I'm dressed for bed.'

'In Bill's dressing-gown.'

'It suits me better than it suits him.' Faye hugged the navy blue, subtly patterned silk and started in the direction of the bedroom.

'Need any help with taking your blood sugar?' offered Belinda.

'I've done it,' Faye smiled. 'Just before you arrived.'

'And?' Tom demanded.

'Eighty.'

'Fine.'

'There's something else I wanted to tell you as well,' Faye added. 'Bill and I talked about the amniocentesis for a long time tonight, and we've decided against it.'

Tom only nodded. 'I thought you might.'

'And does that signify approval, or the reverse?'

'It signifies nothing. It was your decision, and my opinion isn't important.'

'Oh, Tom! You're maddening sometimes. Isn't he?' Faye demanded suddenly of Belinda.

'Younger brothers always are,' she replied sagely, out of deep experience, and was very pleased when, as she had half expected, Tom laughed. That was another nice thing about friendship, wasn't it? Making someone else laugh?

And so it didn't really make sense that when she lay in bed half an hour later, with images of the evening playing themselves chaotically in her mind, her mood was rather blue and wistful. After a friendly evening out like that, capped by a friendly kiss, and Faye's happy news about the baby's movement, surely she ought to be feeling content?

CHAPTER SEVEN

'WHY don't you get your hair cut for Christmas?' Faye suggested to Belinda the day before Christmas Eve. 'You haven't had it done since you came here, and that's nearly four months ago now.'

'It would be cooler for summer,' Belinda acknowledged. 'But could I get an appointment so close to Christmas?'

'Oh, my salon will fit you in,' Faye promised confidently. 'Why don't I phone them now?'

She did so, and was able to get an appointment for two o'clock the following afternoon. 'Which means you'll look gorgeous for Christmas drinks,' said Faye, 'and give your family a lovely surprise on Christmas Day.'

The planned drinks party would be the first time that the Hamiltons had had guests since their party back at the end of August, and the artist was happy and excited about the event. 'It will be everyone from Bill's office, plus other assorted friends. . .and *Tom* of course,' she had explained several days ago.

Belinda didn't know why Faye stressed her brother's name. He came so often to check up on Faye that his presence was hardly cause for special comment, let alone celebration.

'And of course, with a new haircut,' Faye was saying now, 'you'll want to wear something special. Do you have something? Do you want to get something new?'

'Well, no, I'd better not, actually,' Belinda told her timidly, a little bemused by Faye's enthusiasm. 'I've

gone over my budget this month, what with buying
Christmas presents and a new bathing-suit.'

'Oh, yes, you're saving to go overseas. Never mind,
then. I've just thought of the perfect thing to lend you.'

'Oh, don't worry about it, I can easily wear my——'

'No, listen,' said Faye. 'It's never been worn before.
My mother sent it from London and it was just a bit
too big. I was going to have it altered, but now with
the baby it wouldn't fit anyway. It'd be perfect for
tomorrow. Mrs Porter knows where it is in my wardrobe. Let's ring for her and she'll get it right now. No,
on second thoughts, go with her and put it on and
come and show me, there's a love. I'm dying to see
how this will work!'

'Don't ring for Mrs Porter, then, I'll go and get her,'
said Belinda, bowing inevitably to Faye's enthusiasm.

She went to the kitchen, where the dedicated housekeeper was busy making batches of tiny delicacies for
tomorrow's drinks. Mrs Porter was not particularly
pleased at being interrupted by such an errand. It came
under her classification of Faye being 'temperamental',
but she found the dress for Belinda easily enough and
then returned to her canapés.

In her room, Belinda put on the dress with an
uncertain frown. It was certainly gorgeous, and of the
highest quality. Pure silk, as so many of Faye's clothes
were, and shimmeringly black with rich, patterned
beading all over the bustier-style bodice and tiny bolero
jacket. It fitted Belinda perfectly. . .and she acknowledged inwardly that she might have preferred it if it
hadn't. For one thing, she had never worn a strapless
dress before, and although the bodice was tight-fitting
and well supported she couldn't rid herself of the fear
that the dress would go slithering to the floor at some

critical moment, leaving her almost naked, like in a bad dream.

She hoped that perhaps Faye would speak her misgivings aloud that the dress was really far too sophisticated and daring for a humble nurse at her employer's Chirstmas party. But when she returned to the cool breakfast-room where Faye was spending the morning, the artist clapped her hands together delightedly and said, 'There! It fits, and it's fabulous!'

'Are you sure——?'

'Of course you can borrow it. In fact, you can keep it. By the time I can fit into it properly, I'll be a staid old mother of nearly forty strugggling through sleepless nights. In fact, I'll probably *never* feel young enough for that style again. It'll give me a lot of pleasure to see you in it, love, and with the new haircut you'll knock everyone's socks off. I'll enjoy it immensely.'

Faced with Faye's genuine kindness, which surfaced frequently to soften the more ruthless, temperamental side of her personality, Belinda could not admit that she did not feel comfortable in the dress, so she said quite sincerely, 'That's so lovely of you, Faye. I was already looking forward to tomorrow night, and now I will more than ever.'

'I'm sure you will. I have high hopes for the evening.' Faye gave a satisfied, rather cryptic smile that Belinda pondered as she returned to her room to take refuge in more familiar clothing.

Hanging the dress carefully in the wardrobe, though, she did begin to feel excited about tomorrow, a bubbly sort of excitement that wanted to express itself in singing or laughter. Why should this be?

She pondered this question too. It was always nice to see Tom, of course. And Faye planned to show off the eight paintings she had done over the past four months, six of which featured Belinda and all of which were now professionally framed. Belinda was starting to feel a proprietorial sort of pride in Faye's work, especially as her own knowledge of painting increased. She couldn't yet use terms like 'harmony of form' and 'tonal value' with comfort, and she decided that perhaps she didn't want to, but there was something so fresh and vivid about Faye's work, she was starting to love it. . .and even to love each funny figure in each painting that was herself.

So that was why she was excited. Except that, as she stared at her reflection in the big mirror at Pizzazz!, Faye's fashionable hair salon the next afternoon, she knew that this was not the full explanation.

'I'm not sure what to tell them about how I want it done,' she had said to Faye before leaving, running uncertain fingers through the dense yet fluffy waves.

'Don't worry, love,' Faye had told her with authority. 'I've already phoned Miranda and told her what to do. . . That is, if you don't mind my interference.'

'Well, since I have no clear ideas myself. . .'

'Good girl! I promise you, it'll be fabulous. Now go, because Miranda fitted you in specially, and she'll be snappy if you're late. She always is when I am,' Faye had confessed carelessly.

So here Belinda was, with that naked feeling she always got when she looked at her wet hair and towel-draped neck under the bright lights of a salon, and she very much hoped that Faye was right about the end result looking 'fabulous', because she was determined to show everyone at drinks this evening that she was just as *soignée*, just as at ease in a smart social gathering as they were.

Why it should suddenly be important to prove this to a number of people that she hadn't even met, she didn't stop to question, and she firmly suppressed a naggingly persistent image of Tom Russell and Marise Wyspianski last Saturday all dressed up for the annual Christmas ball given by the Coronation Hospital board. They had dropped in to pick up Bill, who was of necessity going without Faye this year, and the sight of Tom in a black dinner suit and a shirt so white that it was almost ultra-violet had rocked Belinda's usual state of equilibrium where their friendship was concerned.

How it had rocked it, she wasn't quite sure. All she knew was that she had been miserable for the rest of the night, and only a teasing conversation with him the next afternoon, when he was dressed very casually in blue jeans and a white T-shirt, had cheered her up again.

'Now, Faye says I'm just to go ahead,' Miranda said crisply, a fortunate intrusion on Belinda's too-circular thoughts.

'Yes, I'm sure I'll like it, whatever you do,' Belinda promised extravagantly.

It was half-past three when she was finally able to survey the result with the aid of mirrors in front and behind.

'It's made an incredible difference,' Miranda assured her.

And that was certainly true. Gone was the natural, below-shoulder, slightly fly-away look, and in its place was a dramatically side-parted bob, which shelved sharply to chin level. It was on the cutting edge of modern style, and was set quite severely in place by generous dollops of mousse and squirts of spray. Belinda knew it would probably look hilarious tomorrow morning if she didn't wash it out tonight.

It *did* look fabulous, Belinda decided firmly, even

though she didn't quite know if that person in the mirror was herself or a professional model.

'Your boyfriend won't recognise you,' Miranda promised.

'Well, my brothers probably won't. They'll probably laugh. . . But I haven't got a boyfriend.'

'Oh, haven't you? That's funny. From what Faye said on the phone. . . I must have got it wrong.'

'I think maybe you did,' Belinda responded timidly.

'It's crazy here at this time of year,' the hairdresser explained. Beringed hands waved in a frenzy around Miranda's own boldly streaked, mane-like hair, and Belinda quickly paid and left, realising she had been very lucky to get squeezed in at the salon when so many women wanted to look special for Christmas.

At home, Faye pronounced herself satisfied with the haircut, but her praise was given absently, and after she had told Belinda to hurry and dress as the guests were due at five, she said too casually, 'And before you go, love, would you get me a couple of Panadols? All the last-minute worry over these guests. . . I've got a bit of a headache.'

'Of course,' Belinda said steadily.

In fact, Faye hadn't had much worry over the cocktail party, as Mrs Porter had prepared everything and all had done smoothly. The artist had had a very quiet day, mainly lying in bed. She hadn't sketched or written letters as she often did. She hadn't even read very much. At the time, Belinda had merely thought she was resting up for the party. Now she was less convinced.

'Are you feeling all right, Faye?'

'I'm fine. '

'How was your after-lunch blood glucose?'

'Oh, a little high, but I've taken care of that.'

'All right,' Belinda conceded, inwardly still wondering if something was wrong. If that was the case, though, why was Faye saying nothing? She was so concerned about her unborn baby, she usually over-reacted to any untoward symptom.

Convincing herself that *she* was now over-reacting, Belinda got the headache tablets, then went to dress, her excitement returning as she put on Faye's dress. With her new hairstyle, as well as make-up, perfume and high-heeled shoes, she felt more confident about herself in the outfit today, and when, just before five o'clock, she found Tom in a lounge-room that was festooned with Christmas reds and greens, she was able to walk across the room to him, confident and smiling.

'Hi, Tom!'

'What on earth have you done to your hair?'

The abrupt question, made after a short, stunned silence, without even the preface of a greeting, was like a slap in the face.

'Oh, I. . .I went to the hairdresser. Doesn't it look any good?'

He studied her for a moment, and she took in his steel-grey, twill-weave trousers and ivory shirt of raw silk. Understated and perfectly tailored, as usual. 'Of course it looks *good*,' he growled at last. 'But I didn't even recognise you for a minute there, and I didn't like the feeling. It looked good before, too.'

'Well, sorry, I can't get it glued back on,' she said crisply, and saw his rueful smile.

'Sorry.' He reached out and touched her shoulder briefly, the warmth of his fingers travelling instantly through the beaded silk to set her skin, so sensitive to his touch for some reason, on fire. 'I've been tactless. I wasn't expecting a miraculous transformation, you see, I was expecting the Belinda I've come to know and love.' He said the last word lightly, and they both knew he didn't mean it. 'That dress is new, too, isn't it?' He was frowning again.

'Yes, Faye gave it to me.'

'Very glamorous.' But it was a tersely worded compliment, and as he turned to take an olive from the tray of hors-d'oeuvres already laid out on a side-table, her stabbing disappointment told Belinda that he was the person she had really dressed up for today, though what she wanted to prove to him she didn't quite know.

'How's Faye?' he asked. It was a relief to both of them to return to this familiar territory.

'She says she's fine.'

'What do you mean, *says* she's fine?'

'I'm sure she *is* fine. It's just that she had a headache and was a bit reticent about it, which is unlike her. I suppose she's worried that it won't be gone before the guests arrive. . .and they'll be starting to come soon.'

'What do you mean, *starting* to come?' he demanded indignantly. 'I'm here already, aren't I? And I'm a guest.'

'Oh, you don't count,' Belinda responded frankly, enjoying the shout of laughter that sprang ot his lips.

'Well, I did come early to check on Faye,' he admitted. 'Is she in her room?'

'I think so. She should be dressed for the party by now.'

And at that moment Faye herself came into the lounge, in a pretty sleeveless floral dress gathered loosely into a low waist below the growing bulge of the baby. She was due on March the nineteenth, and had reached the twenty-eighth week of her pregnancy. At this point, the start of the third trimester, the baby would have a chance of survival outside the womb, although no one was anxious for it to make an early appearance.

'So, Tom, what do you think of our new Belinda?' Faye asked her brother archly as soon as they had exchanged a brief kiss in greeting.

'Very nice,' was his growled response. 'It was your idea, I suppose?'

'Oh, Tom! You're not going to be like that, are you?' Faye protested.

'Like what?'

'Just difficult. Yes, it was my idea, and yes, I sent her to my salon, and yes, I'm the bossiest person in the world, as you used to say when you were nine, but does that make the finished result any less attractive? She could be a model tonight, couldn't she?'

'I'll grant you that, certainly, and she's never looked like a model before.' The way Tom said it, it didn't sound like a compliment.

'Oh, lord, you're going to be in a bad mood all evening, now, aren't you?' Faye exclaimed, after an anxious glance at Belinda, her bright mouth creasing into two thin lines. 'I want Belinda to look her best so that——' She broke off. 'Never mind—I just wanted her to look her best. Is that so terrible?'

'No, it's very commendable, Faye, but——'

'I'm going in to the kitchen to see how Mrs Porter's getting on,' Belinda announced firmly, cutting off Tom's words. 'Let me know when you've finished arguing about me, and I'll come back.'

'No, Belinda——'

'Please, love——'

The two voices came in unison, but she ignored them, simply turning to smile back at Faye and Tom from the doorway. 'It's all right. I know how much you two enjoy a good tiff, and I seem to provide a convenient topic for it. But for me it's a bit like a tennis match—I get tired of turning my head from side to side listening to you.'

She tried to leave, but Tom crossed the room in two strides and took her arm. 'You've made your point,' he growled. 'And we're sorry—*I'm* sorry. And I'm sorry about this idiotic issue of how you look. You look great. I'm glad Faye made you do it, all right?'

'She didn't *make* me!' said Belinda crossly.

'Didn't she?'

'No!'

'Hmm. . .' He narrowed his eyes sceptically, but said no more about it. They heard a car in the driveway, then the sound of footsteps rasping on brick paving, and the hum of a second car.

'Already!' murmured Faye. 'I must tell Mrs Porter to——'

'First, Faye,' Tom broke in, 'Belinda tells me you have a headache.'

'Not any more. I took some pills.'

'And you feel fine?'

'Of course I feel fine. I'm just a little tense about the party, and it's been so *hot*!'

'Yes, a lot of pregnant women feel hot in the last months,' he agreed, still studying her closely. 'You'll want to keep the air-conditioning working pretty hard this summer. No other symptoms? Any swelling?'

'My hands and feet a bit, but that's usual for me in hot weather.'

'Still. . .   Blood-pressure normal on Monday at your appointment?'

'Yes, apparently.'

'Well, if that headache comes back, or if anything else happens. . .'

Faye nodded seriously, biting her lower lip. 'I know.

I'm sure it's nothing, though.' Her voice was high. 'The party. . . I'll lie down on the couch again as soon as I've seen Mrs Porter.'

'Yoo-hoo! Merry Christmas! Where's the mistletoe and someone to kiss? Hey, don't tell me I'm the first to arrive?' It was Greg Carey, and as if his entrance was a cue for everyone else to appear, the Christmas Eve cocktail party was in full swing within ten minutes.

'Actually, I'm extremely disappointed that there's no mistletoe,' Greg drawled.

'You'll have to complain to the host and hostess,' Belinda answered lightly. 'I'm afraid I'm not responsible.'

It was two hours later, and the sprawling house was still loud with laughter and voices, and crammed with people. The early arrivals had been taken out to the studio to look at Faye's work, but then things had got too hectic, and now the highly praised paintings were forgotten.

This party was a much bigger affair than the small gathering back in August, and Belinda had been swept along on a tide of food and drink and conversation. She was beginning to be afraid, in fact, that she had drunk too much. A brandy Alexander, a glass of white wine—and she suspected now that the orange juice she held in her hand wasn't just orange juice at all. Greg had brought it from the side-table for her.

'I think you might have got this drink from the wrong tray,' she said to him now. 'I might just take it out to the kitchen and pour another one, if you don't mind. I think this has got quite a bit of vodka in it.'

'Oh, dear, how terrible! How naughty! How wicked!' Grey exclaimed mockingly, and she flushed and drew away stiffly.

He had been monopolising her for most of the evening, or trying to, and she was growing less and less happy about it. At first, admittedly, she had been flattered. He was a very successful, very good-looking professional in his mid-thirties—just as Tom Russell was, although that was irrelevant, of course—and to find that he seemed to be interested in *her* was satisfying somehow.

Was it her new haircut, and Faye's dress? She started to feel much more comfortable about how she looked, and unconsciously began to relax and to hold herself in the quietly poised way she did when dressed in a nurse's uniform or casual clothes.

But as the evening advanced, she wished she hadn't let Greg guess that she was pleased at his attention. Twice she made the kind of excuse that people made at cocktail parties when they wanted to extricate themselves from a conversation and move on to talk with another guest, but five minutes later he was back at her side again, bending closer and closer towards her so that she became unpleasantly aware of the stale, alcoholic aura of his breath.

He seemed obtuse, as she felt by this time that she had more than cancelled out any slight encouragement she might have given him at first.

And now he was talking about mistletoe, and she didn't have to be very sophisticated or experienced to realise that he was angling quite unsubtly for a chance to kiss her. He wasn't going to be fobbed off by the issue of her drink either, she found.

'Shall I tell you a secret?' he was saying. 'I got you a vodka and orange on purpose.'

'And why did you do that?'

From long experience, Belinda's younger brothers would have known in an instant by the crisp, deceptively mild tone that she was no longer fooling around, but unfortunately Greg Carey wasn't possessed of this experience, so he said on a thick, purring note, 'Because you need to loosen up, get rid of some inhibitions. I want to help you. And alcohol makes that sort of loosening happen very smoothly.'

'As you know from personal experience?'

He laughed. 'Sure! Now. . .' And he bent towards her and extracted a kiss from her reluctant lips the way he might have taken the pit from an apricot.

Some people might like such kisses, Belinda thought. She hoped so, for Greg's sake. *She* certainly didn't like them, however. 'Don't do that again, please,' she said, her gaze quickly flicking through the room to see who had noticed. One or two people perhaps, but they didn't seem interested, and they weren't Tom Russell. In fact, he wasn't even in the room at the moment, thank goodness, and Bill was absorbed in conversation. She couldn't see Faye either. No one to tell tales, then.

For the moment, she didn't stop to wonder why she would have been so distressed if Tom *had* seen that unpleasant kiss. She didn't have time to wonder about anything.

'Don't "*do that*"?' Greg was saying, in falsetto imitation of her own tone—although again he hadn't caught the ominous undercurrent to her words. 'Then shall I do this? Or this?' He bent to her again and nibbled her ear, then held her jaw in his hands and delivered a kiss that was heavy and almost insolent.

For a moment, the thought raced through her head, He hardly knows me. He doesn't even like me, not really. Why is he doing this? To punish me because he can see I don't want to?

Then her anger erupted, her hand flashed upwards and she had delivered a stinging slap to his left cheek

before she even realised that she intended to. Horrified
. . .and yet strangely relieved and satisfied, and tingling
with primitive energy and release, she turned on her
heel and threaded so nimbly through the crowded
guests that she reached the French doors that opened
on to the side veranda before Greg had recovered
enough to take a single step.

Daring to pause in the doorwsay to take stock of the
reaction her dramatic gesture had produced, she found
that only those closest to herself and Greg had even
noticed. Perversely, she wished now that Tom *had*
been in the room after all. She felt sometimes that he
didn't know how spirited she could be, and this would
certainly have shown him! A large group in the
opposite corner had erupted into laughter at just the
right moment, to mask the sound of her action, however, and even those who had seen and heard were
simply hiding slightly shocked and curious smiles
behind polite hands and pretending to go on with their
talk.

There was to be no stunned silence, no aghast staring
and, it seemed, no dramatic response from Greg.
Thank goodness! All the same, she badly needed some
air and solitude, so she stepped out to the veranda,
closed the door silently behind her, slipped off her high
heels and held them in one hand, then padded on silent
stockinged feet down the back stairs and into the
garden.

Dispensing with the paths that snaked through half a
dozen different garden realms, she brushed through
the shrubbery, feeling a little wild in the wake of her
primitive gesture. That horrible slightly tipsy feeling
had gone now too, which was a relief. Perhaps it had
just been the rather stuffy air in that crowded room. It
was so peaceful out here in contrast, and so redolent

of nature's life. The warm, tropical earth gave off the sweet, pungent odour of mingled bloom and decay, and the leaves rustled like independent creatures.

Wait a minute, though. There *was* a creature, an animal in the bushes ahead, wasn't there? Belinda came to a silent halt and peered in front of her. The sun had just set, and the sky was still light and glowing with softly pastel mauves and pinks, but here in the thick trees, it was hard to see. She caught a glimpse of colour—dark red—and realised it was a woman's dress.

Then she heard a high, effusive whisper. 'It isn't mistletoe, but will it do?'

A slight sudden puff of breeze lifted a thickly leafed branch in front of her and she saw two figures, framed by the foliage at the instant their lips met in a long, smooth, seductive and very mutual kiss. Then the breeze died and the branch sighed and sank again.

On feet that tried desperately to be silent, Belinda crept away, not stopping or turning round until she reached the looming mass of the house. Greg Carey and his distasteful kiss were forgotten, were unimportant. The picture she had just seen was engraved in her mind like a photograph, and even such a short glimpse of the two lovers had left her in no doubt about their identity. The woman's sleek cap of dark hair and the bold colour of her dress. . . The man's clean, confident profile and broad, capable shoulders. . .

Marise and Tom.

CHAPTER EIGHT

THERE was nothing Belinda could do about the way she felt. It simply had to be endured. On legs that moved numbly and automatically, she climbed the back stairs again and went through the kitchen back to the party. It had taken pain and misery to tell her what she had not learned from happiness—that she was in love with Tom Russell.

'I should have known,' she whispered fiercely to herself. 'Being so happy with him. . .and just thinking about him. . .over these past few months, should have told me. I must be a fool to have needed to see him and Marise together like that before I knew.'

Obscurely, she felt that if only she *had* known before things might have been different, but then common sense told her that yes, things might have been different: probably they would have been worse. The comfortable feeling of friendship she had had since that night in August, when she had so firmly suppressed her teenage-flavoured infatuation, was what had allowed love to grow.

She didn't even know at what point friendship had turned into love, and if she had realised it when it happened the new bud of feeling might have blossomed crazily into hopeless longing and tongue-tied need. . . or perhaps it would have frosted away and died. She supposed wearily that she should be hoping this last thing would still happen, should be *making* it happen if it didn't happen on its own, but she knew that however hopeless this love for him was, it was the most precious and valuable thing she had ever experienced.

Feeling years older than when she woke up this morning—and not just because she had acquired a new, sophisticated façade of hair and clothing during the day—Belinda plunged into the middle of the party crowd again.

Needing something light and refreshing to slake a newly parched mouth and throat, she squirted soda from a siphon into a tall glass and added a cluster of ice cubes. She took several long mouthfuls of the drink, then looked around for Faye, wanting to make sure this party wasn't too taxing for her patient.

But Faye wasn't reclined on the couch that she had declared would be her home base for the evening, and with a sudden pang of anxiety Belinda realised that she hadn't seen or talked to Faye since about half-past five. It was now. . .she caught a glimpse of a man's gold watch as his hand reached for a drink, and saw to her consternation that it was already after eight.

Finding Bill on the far side of the room, she went up to him and asked without preamble, 'Where's Faye?'

'Well, she went to lie down about an hour ago. . .'

'She took her insulin at the right time, and ate properly?'

'Yes, I brought her the tray Mrs Porter had set out for her in the kitchen. She was worried that she wouldn't have an accurate idea of what she ate if she just picked and nibbled. When she'd finished she said she needed some peace and quiet for a while. That was at half-past six.'

'It's after eight now,' said Belinda worriedly. 'That's over an hour and a half, and I haven't checked on her. Why didn't she tell me she was going to lie down?'

'She didn't want to disturb you,' Bill frowned, rumpling his wavy, greying hair. 'You were very busy talking to Greg Carey. She was finding the party more trying than she expected, and told me to come and get her if I needed her for anything. . . But you're right, time has got away from me. Let's go!'

He pulled her from the room and together they went to the master suite. The ivory damask curtains were drawn and Faye's body was just a hump in the darkness. She stirred as they entered and gave a creaking groan as she began to waken.

'Are you all right, Faye?' Belinda asked, as Faye opened her eyes. Bill drew the curtains to let in the last of the twilight, then, as Faye's eyes began to adjust, he turned to two low antique glass lamps.

'I'm fine,' she said dazedly, then added on a different note, 'Actually, my head's pounding. What's the time?'

'Eight o'clock.'

'I've really been asleep. I feel. . .very queasy and my stomach is cramping.' She sat up with difficulty and began to take gulps of air. 'What's happening? Look at my hands!'

She held them out and Belinda saw that the normally slender fingers were fat and bloated. The symptoms, only hinted at by a headache earlier that could easily have been nothing, and by mild swelling that was normal in hot weather, had intensified with frightening suddenness, and Belinda was in no doubt about what it meant.

Toxaemia. Pre-eclampsia. Two names for the same condition that was once life-threatening to both mother and baby but could now easily be brought under control—if warning signs were heeded in time.

'I need to get to the bathroom,' Faye said thickly, holding a hand to her mouth.

'Stay there!' ordered Belinda. 'I'll bring you a bowl.

Bill, call the hospital and tell them we're coming in. And find Tom. He's. . .he's in the garden with Marise, down near the fern rockery. Don't worry about being tactful when you interrupt them.'

Bill left the room, and immediately afterwards it became clear that it was too late to bring a bowl for Faye. She was miserably sick into her best mono-grammed towel, and although this made the sharpness of the headache diminish for the moment Belinda was convinced that the diagnosis of toxaemia was the correct one.

She brought water, a fresh towel and a wet flannel for Faye, then helped her to lie back on her left side. Next she got a blood-pressure cuff, with its attached meter, and took a quick reading, to find that, as she had feared, Faye's blood-pressure was significantly higher than it should be.

'I need to weigh you, Faye,' she said.

'Weigh me? At a time like this?' groaned Faye.

'It'll tell us if that swelling is potentially dangerous. Tom will want to know.'

'All right,' Faye sighed.

'Stay there while I bring the bathroom scales,' ordered Belinda.

A minute later she had the result, and although the scales were less accurate than those at Dr Greene's consulting-rooms, the weight gain still seemed to be dramatic.

'Almost three kilograms!' Faye exclaimed. 'Since Monday?'

'I know. It's not normal,' said Belinda. 'It's caused by water retention, not by what you ate. Tom will want to check for proteinuria and test your reflexes, but even if those things are normal he and Dr Greene may want to pop you in hospital for a while.'

'I'm not going to lose the baby?'

'No, definitely not!' Belinda said firmly. No point in alarming and stressing Faye further with worst-case scenarios. 'But we do have to take this condition seriously and get it under control.'

Faye didn't reply. She had returned to bed and Belinda could see that she was making an enormous effort to remain calm. Remembering how responsive Faye's blood glucose level was to stress, she was about to monitor its level, but, as she got out the kit, Tom arrived, his tall figure catapulting into the room and only a slight untidiness to his dark hair betraying the fact that he had so recently been locked in Marise's arms in the garden.

'Bill's calling the hospital now,' he told her.

'An ambulance?' Belinda asked briefly.

'No.' He shook his head impatiently. 'It's not as urgent as that, fortunately. We'll drive her. We have the equipment here to test for proteinuria, don't we?'

'Yes.'

'Then let's get a sample straight away. Don't get up, Faye, your job is to *rest*. Belinda, bring a bedpan.'

Five minutes later he had read the result, and said on a controlled sigh, 'Yes, there is some. Not much.'

His glance flicked to Belinda and there was a moment of wordless professional understanding. Proteinuria meant kidney damage, and that was something Faye, whose diabetes stressed her kidneys in any case, could not afford to continue with. If the condition was mild, then the damage should not be lasting, but every delay increased the stress on Faye's kidneys. . .and on the rest of her body.

Tom's quick testing of her tendon reflexes revealed their characteristic briskness, and both the medical professionals realised that the condition was progressing, when they had been hoping against all the evidence that it would not.

Bill and Tom carried Faye to the car, while Belinda hurried to change. Almost wrenching off the fragile beaded jacket, and unfastening the strapless dress so that it plummeted to the floor, she grabbed the first garments she found—light pink cotton trousers and a grey and white striped cotton blouse—then forced her feet into flat leather sandals without stopping to undo and refasten the thin buckled straps.

As she raced through the lounge to join Tom and Faye in the car, she saw the party guests, who had sensed that something was amiss but had not yet been told the details, milling and exclaiming in the background, like flocks of frightened birds. Greg Carey was there near the door, and when he reached out to grab her arm, asking, 'What's going on?' she shook him off impatiently and didn't even see his face close and tighten in anger at her second rejection of the evening.

She met Bill coming back up the steps, and they did not waste time on speech. He was staying behind to explain the situation tactfully and bring the party to an end, and Belinda was sure that no one would object to leaving—with the possible exception of Greg. The atmosphere was alive with concern over Faye now, and the telephone would be ringing hot later on as people wanted to know how she was. . .

'What are you holding, Belinda?' asked Tom as he reversed rapidly down the driveway. They were in Bill's roomy Mercedes, and Bill would follow later in Tom's own sports car, which had not been practical for transporting Faye in complete comfort.

'The glucose testing kit. . .' she said rather blankly, not quite understanding how it could still be in her hands. 'I was going to take a reading, but there wasn't time. I suppose I picked it up in my room instead of my handbag.'

'What was your post-dinner reading, Faye?' asked Tom.

'I. . .I didn't take one,' Faye told him. 'I was a bit late with my insulin injection tonight, and then I gulped my meal because I wanted to lie down. . .'

'Damn it, Faye, you've really lost control today!'

Without thinking about how he might interpret the gesture, Belinda put a warning hand heavily on Tom's knee. His sister didn't need anger at the moment, and it was only his concern that had allowed it to escape. Control *yourself*! the hot pressure of her palm said frankly.

'Sorry, Faye,' he muttered at once. 'That was unnecessary.'

'It's my fault,' Belinda began. 'I should never have gone to the hairdresser——'

'Please!' Tom seemed angry again. 'Enough of the subject. It's not doing anyone any good. Faye. . .?'

But there was no reply, and when Belinda turned from the front passenger seat to look at the artist stretched out in the back, she saw that Faye had the back of her hand pressed against her mouth to stifle her sobs. Heedless of seatbelt regulations, she leaned across and gripped her shoulder.

'It's all right, Faye!' she said urgently. 'It's going to be all right. We can easily bring this condition under control. You *must* relax! Let me tell you. . .let me tell you. . .' she racked her brains '. . .about the time the twins thought they'd found gold in the creek on our farm. It was about a year before we moved to Brisbane, so they must only have been about eight years old. An old stockman who lived nearby had a gold-pan and a sluice-box—not to mention a very dubious prospector's map, with "reef gold" marked in the most enticing, most improbable places, and they got a bad case of gold fever. So one day. . .'

She talked on, making the anecdote as interesting and amusing as she possibly could, encouraged by Faye's subsiding sobs and by the enigmatic silence from the frowning driver of the car. At the end, when she told about the enterprising boys' attempt to send a sample 'nugget'—of worthless pyrites—to the mines department for assaying, Faye actually smiled, and quickly Belinda went on to think of more stories from her outback childhood.

She was still talking about the snake that lived under the water tank when Tom swung the wheel and purred rapidly up the hospital driveway, and if his face was still set in a grim frown and he didn't seem to be listening to her words at all, she shouldn't have minded, because the object of the exercise had been to entertain Faye, not him.

She *did* mind, though, and, as they were met at the emergency entrance with a wheeled stretcher-bed for Faye and a paged message for Tom summoning him to the renal unit to attend urgently to another patient, her concern for Faye's condition battled for priority in her thoughts with painful images of Marise Wyspianski glowing in the magic aura of Tom's kiss, and of Tom himself, at the wheel of the Mercedes just moments ago, staring so grimly into the Christmas Eve traffic. Was he wishing he was still with Marise? That she was here beside him now, instead of his sister's nurse? It seemed all too likely.

'The obstetrics and gynaecology team will take over from here,' he explained tersely. 'I have to go. I'll be up to see you as soon as I can. Belinda, wait in the foyer and I'll take you home afterwards.'

'Can't I——?' she began, but Faye interrupted more urgently.

'No, Tom, I want her to come up with me! She can, can't she? She has to—I'm so used to having her now.'

Belinda saw Tom's quick, questioning glance in her direction, but she ignored it. 'Of course I'll come up with you, Faye. I'll stay till Bill gets here. Longer, if you want me to.'

Tom gave a slow, satisfied nod and left them after a last reassuring pat on Faye's shoulder. She was wheeled to the lift, with Belinda at her side, and it felt strange and yet very familiar to be plunged into the atmosphere of a large hospital again after four months away. Not just *any* large hospital either, but Coronation, the place where she had trained and worked for almost five years.

There was the same impossibly perfect shine on the vinyl-tiled floors, the same echoing clunk as the lift began its smooth acceleration up the shaft, the same clean yet sometimes over-strong smell of lemon disinfectant, the same sense of drama and importance overlaid by the deceptive tranquillity of the wards.

Today, however, she wasn't taking the familiar route up to the endocrine ward, with the familiar reluctant realisation that Deana Davenport would probably be on her shift. And something else was different, too— her feelings for Tom. The new awareness of her love for him stabbed again at her heart.

Was it her heart? It was more like a huge, heavy lump in her throat, and it was certainly painful. How could she have been foolish enough to let it happen? she asked herself inwardly as the lift slowed and stopped, and its wide metal doors sighed open. Here at the hospital, she had been so realistic about it, had known it could never develop into anything real. But the luxurious tropical oasis that was the Hamiltons' house, and the fact that she saw Tom every day and had become friends with him, had led her to drop her guard without fully realising that she had done so, and now she was utterly vulnerable to him.

'Which room?' the orderly said to a nurse at the desk that oversaw the entrance to the ward.

'Twenty,' answered the young redhead, not someone Belinda knew, even by sight. She guessed that, during her four months away, there had been staff coming and going as always.

Faye was wheeled to the small private room further along the corridor, and two nurses came immediately to help her into bed and take routine observations. Belinda said hello to one of them, Judy Stack, whom she knew from the nurses' home, then sat on a rather uncomfortable chair in the corner as Faye was examined by a junior obstetrician.

'Dr Greene is on his way,' Dr Petersen promised.

'What are you giving her?' Belinda whispered to Judy as the latter prepared a syringe on the doctor's order.

'Phenobarbitol, for the moment.'

'What was her blood-pressure?'

Judy told Belinda the reading, and Belinda nodded. Slightly higher than the measurement she had taken at home.

'And can you take a blood-sugar reading as soon as possible, as well?' she asked Judy.

'I've got the kit ready. We were told on the phone about her diabetes. You've been her nurse at home for four months?'

'That's right,' said Belinda.

'How is it? I've heard private patients can be hell.'

'No, not at all, in this case,' Belinda said staunchly,

and she could see that Judy was a little disappointed at not hearing any juicy anecdotes.

It *wasn't* hell working for Faye, and as she sat there waiting for the medical staff to leave the artist's room, Belinda realised, I've changed. When I come back here . . .if I do. . .I'm not going to be so timid and unsure. I've experienced more now, and it's going to stand me in good stead.

Some minutes later, after a visit from Dr Greene, who pronounced Faye's condition to be 'quite satisfactory', but ordered a follow-up blood glucose test in an hour, as the level was somewhat higher than it should have been, Belinda was left alone with her patient.

'Close the door, will you, love?' Faye said at once. 'And tell me what's going on. I feel so tired! I'll rest my eyes, if you don't mind.' She lay back with a hand lightly covering her closed lids.

'Yes, just rest completely, Faye,' Belinda agreed, as she pressed the door home with a gentle click. 'Dr Greene seems fairly pleased. Your body should be getting itself back to normal soon.'

'But can something still go wrong?'

'The worst that can happen. . .' she took a deep breath, hoping that this was the right thing to say '. . .is that the baby has to be delivered over the next few days.'

'Delivered? But. . .'

'An emergency Caesarean, probably. I know it would be premature, but at twenty-eight weeks there's a very good chance of survival, and with every day of your pregnancy that passes, that chance improves.'

'Then I have to stay here in hospital and just wait for this toxaemia thing to develop?' asked Faye anxiously.

'No, I'm sure you'll be able to go home in a few

days. Do you understand what's happening to your body?'

'Yes, my kidneys are over-producing a hormone called renin.'

'That's right. It's the kidneys' response to the water retention you've started having. The renin raises your blood-pressure, which in turn leads to more kidney stress and more water retention, and on into the more severe symptoms. It's a vicious cycle.'

'And what stops it?'

'Well, Dr Greene has prescribed magnesium sulphate if your blood-pressure hasn't dropped soon, but as long as you rest, you've got a very good chance of reversing the cycle.'

'So when I get home—if I do. . .'

'I'm afraid it will be tougher, yes,' Belinda admitted. 'We have to do everything to stop this from recurring.'

'No more parties, then?'

'No, I shouldn't think so.'

'Or lying on the couch.'

'No, Dr Greene will probably insist on complete bed-rest now.'

'Sometimes I wonder if it's really worth it!' Faye broke out rebelliously, with a negativity that Belinda had not seen in her for months. 'Why did I think I wanted a baby? Look what it's doing to me! And what if the baby isn't all right? Why did I kid myself that I'd ever get there successfully in my condition?'

'But you *are* nearly there, Faye,' Belinda said coaxingly. 'This is a setback, but it's under control now.'

'How did I let it happen? I must have known——' Faye broke off.

'Well,' Belinda responded carefully, 'you were busy, and——'

'Never mind, never mind. Thinking about it isn't

going to help now.' Faye opened her eyes for a moment and stared into space, then carefully closed them again. 'Let's talk about something else.' She shifted restlessly, but didn't speak.

Belinda waited quietly, sensing her patient's need for distraction, but wanting to take a cue from Faye herself before launching into shallow chat. Outside, there were the usual hospital sounds—ambulant patients moving about the ward in slippers, nurses talking at the nurses' station, the distant squeaking wheel of a cleaner's trolley—but in here it was very quiet. What Faye said next, though, was the last thing Belinda had expected.

'Tell me, how is Tom treating you these days?'

'*Treating* me?' echoed Belinda.

'Yes. I mean, you're friends, aren't you? You always seem to be.'

'I. . .I think so. I hope so.'

'Hmm. . .' There was a pause, and Faye moved again, settling herself lower in the bed and taking her hand from her eyes. She lay there with them closed, but was clearly far from sleep. 'Has he told you about his divorce?'

Belinda's throat tightened suddenly. 'No. . .' It came out huskily and she cleared her throat quickly, to say in a light, clear tone which she hoped betrayed nothing, 'He didn't even tell me about his marriage!'

'No, I didn't think so,' said Faye. 'He doesn't talk about it. But I thought you should know.' She didn't explain why.

There was a tap at the door and Judy Stack came in again, her coffee-brown curls bouncing. 'Time for another blood-pressure reading,' she said. 'Sorry to interrupt.'

'Already?' sighed Faye.

'Yes, Dr Greene has ordered quarter-hourly observations at first. We'll see how this goes.' Judy took the reading quickly and expertly, then announced with satisfaction, 'It's dropped. Only slightly, but it *has* dropped! That's great!' She noted the reading on Faye's chart, clipped to the end of the bed, then ducked out apologetically, closing her door behind her.

'Does that mean the worst is over?' Faye wanted to know.

'It's a good sign,' Belinda replied cautiously, and there was a small silence, then Faye spoke again.

'We were talking about Tom.'

'Were we?' said Belinda, her voice far too high. She flushed and looked down quickly as she caught Faye's curious, narrow-eyed glance.

'You know we were, love,' Faye said gently, as she lay back against the pillows again. 'I'd just told you he was divorced.'

'I *would* like to hear about it,' Belinda admitted. 'But not tonight. You're tired.'

'Let me talk,' Faye pleaded wearily. 'It helps me to stop thinking about all this.' Her expansive gesture took in the room with its warm yet institutional curtains and modern yet inevitably cold and clinical equipment. 'I really hate being in hospital,' she confessed superfluously.

'I know,' Belinda nodded soothingly. 'Talk, then.' But she wondered uneasily how long it would be before Tom himself finished with his patient over on the other ward and came back here.

'He was very young,' Faye began, 'and she was very ambitious. An actress—Sylvia Leigh. You might have heard of her. She went to London and is doing very well now.'

'Sylvia Leigh. . . Yes, I *have* heard of her,' Belinda

murmured, wondering painfully all over again how she could have let Tom capture her heart. She was a nurse who had never been kissed, and he had been married to a sensational young actress. The contrast was almost ludicrous.

'Well, they were infatuated with each other at first. That's all it ever was, I think,' Faye mused. 'They never really knew each other. She thought a young, rising doctor was glamorous as well as secure, but she didn't have an atom of real interest in his work. And Tom loves his work.'

'I know,' Belinda agreed absently, unaware of Faye's sudden glance in her direction.

'Tom, in turn, was very smug about having captured such a beautiful woman. I'm his sister, so I can be blunt about it. He *was* smug, unbearably so, for a while. But that soon wore off. They fought a lot, which she loved, and he hated.'

'How do you mean?' asked Belinda, appalled.

'Oh, you know the sort of thing. Very actressy— flinging plates, storming out of other people's dinner parties. People say *I'm* temperamental, but at least I try not to be! Sylvia loved creating as loud a scene as possible, and at least half of it was just a performance. Tom used to go white and silent at first, and then end up shouting back in sheer self-defence.'

'It sounds horrible,' Belinda murmured.

'It was,' said Faye. 'I think that's why he hasn't remarried, although it's been ten years now. . . Then she started having an affair.'

'I suppose it was inevitable,' Belinda remarked.

'For her, yes. Tom would have had to be pushed a lot further before he would have done it. If I can say he's smug because I'm his sister, I can also say he's a man of very high principles.'

'Is he. . .?' Belinda picked unseeingly at her fingers in her lap.

'I knew about the affair before he did,' Faye went on over Belinda's mumured comment. 'That was awful! I didn't know whether to tell him or. . . It was the producer of a touring play from England, and she thought he'd help her to launch her career in England . . .which of course he did. So she left Tom and went to London, there was a very clinical divorce, and that was that. Sylvia's divorced from Gordon Sheare now too. Perhaps he ceased to be useful to her once she'd had some success in England—I don't know. But that's the whole story as far as Tom's concerned.'

'And they never had children?' Belinda asked carefully.

'No, thank goodness.' Faye patted her growing belly as if already determined to shield her own child from the pain of something like a divorce. 'It didn't last long enough for that. One day he'll want some, I'm sure, when he meets the right person.'

There was silence for a moment, and the sounds of the hospital intruded again briefly, then Belinda blurted, 'What made you feel that I needed to know about it, Faye?'

But before the other woman could respond, there was a confident rap at the door and it opened to admit Tom himself, looking harried and slightly out of breath. He stopped short as the two women stared up at him, and suddenly an expression of relief washed the tension from his strongly chiselled features. A smile touched his lips.

'You've been gossiping, haven't you?' he accused teasingly.

'A teeny bit,' Faye admitted, summoning a smile.

'Then I take it Dr Greene wasn't too concerned?'

'Well, he was, of course,' said Belinda, 'but he only gave phenobarbitol, no magnesium sulphate yet, and her blood-pressure has dropped slightly already.

'Good, then there's every hope that the condition will ebb of its own accord now, as long as you rest properly. Thank goodness, Faye!'

'I know!' she said on a high note. 'When can I go home?'

'They'll be doing another blood glucose test soon, though,' Belinda put in. 'That was a little high before.'

'Hmm, yes. I'd better check that the nursing staff are up to date on her meal and insulin timetable.'

'What about your other patient, Tom?' asked Faye, moving gingerly in the bed.

He grimaced. 'Not too good, I'm afraid—I did everything I could for the moment, but his kidney failure is almost complete. I'll be in again first thing in the morning to see him, so I'll be able to come and wish you a Merry Christmas, Faye.'

'Christmas!' both Belinda and Faye exclaimed at once.

'Forget, did you?' Tom left the room on a laugh and went out to the nurses' station, almost bumping into Bill Hamilton on the way.

'It took me a hell of a long time to get everyone to go,' Faye's husband said explosively as he strode into the room. 'They all began offering to help, offering this, offering that. I finally said the only thing I damn well wanted was for them to leave so I could get to the hospital. Greg Carey had had *far* too much to drink!'

He buried his face in his wife's shoulder, then kissed her tenderly, and Belinda slid soundlessly from her chair and out of the room, closing the door behind her. Faye would have no further need of her tonight.

Indeed, she was starting to wonder—in a moment of forlornness that was unlike her—if anyone needed her at all.

The nurses on this ward had to be primarily responsible for Faye's care while she was here, and Belinda must not risk treading on their professional toes, although she would tell Judy Stack that she was available whenever they had questions. At home, Mrs Jelbart had done all the Christmas preparations this year—the cake and pudding, the mince pies, the decorations, the turkey and the tree. Belinda hadn't even managed to get out there to put all her packages beneath the tree yet. She would have to do it tomorrow when she arrived for Christmas lunch just before noon. It made her feel more like a guest than a family member.

Worst of all, perhaps, was the realisation that Tom didn't need her. She had been tricking herself earlier into thinking that he did, that their friendship was nearly as important to him as it was to her, but seeing him in the garden with Marise tonight, and hearing about his marriage, unhappy though it had been, had made her realise that friendship was never as important as passion—at least, she was sure, not to a man.

She watched him as she stood outside Faye's hospital room, and thought what a thoroughly manly man he was too. He was standing at the nurses' station, leaning one elbow casually on the high desk as he talked to Judy Stack. From this distance she could see how broad his shoulders were, and how strong and compact were his hips above those long thighs. It was getting quite late now, and the ward had already been darkened for the night. Lamps lighting the desks at the nurses' station were the brightest things in this open central space, and one of the lamps was catching Tom's hair in its light, giving the short locks a golden glow like a halo, and bringing his commanding profile into sharp focus.

Above him, the ward's Christmas decorations looped in colours of green, red, silver, gold and white, and his elbow threatened to knock over a small ornamental tree hung with miniature packages. She heard Judy's laugh, wondered if Tom had teased her, and guessed that the other nurse was less than immune to his charms. She remembered what Deana Davenport's friend had said four months ago—'If I had a dollar for every nurse. . .who's been infatuated with Tom Russell. . .'

And that was how her love for him felt at the moment—as cheap and useless as a dollar.

He turned and saw her. 'Hi! Almost finished. . .

'Oh, it's all right. I'll take a taxi,' she told him.

'To your family's? Is that where you're going?'

'No, but——'

'Then no more arguments. I'll drop you home. At the Hamiltons', that is,' he added, as if to remind her how temporary her home with Faye and Bill was.

'All right, then,' she conceded, realising that it would seem odd if she went on refusing his offer.

'Don't hesitate to page me,' he said, turning back to Judy. 'And make that clear to the next shift as well. Especially if it's a diabetic issue rather than an obstetric one.'

'Of course, Doctor,' murmured Judy, gazing up at him through the dark crescents of her attractively long lashes.

'See you tomorrow, then.'

'Yes.' The nurse smiled at him, then glanced quickly at Belinda, and the latter was certain she saw envy in the glance.

She has nothing to be envious of, if only she knew, Belinda thought wearily.

With little desire to talk, she walked beside Tom to his car—the sports car this time, as he had exchanged keys with Bill a few minutes ago. Tom evidently didn't want conversation either, so both were silent. He didn't even speak as he opened the passenger door for her, but when they were both seated inside, he didn't start the engine, simply sat there instead, gazing out over the slightly sloping and now largely empty car park.

Belinda risked a cautious glance at him, but met only an unreadable profile. He had his hands clasped behind his head and was leaning against the head-rest behind him so that his tanned throat was exposed. He sighed heavily, and Belinda was about to ask what was wrong —after all, they were still friends, in spite of what she had seen in the garden tonight, and her revelation of feeling shouldn't dictate this new reticence—when he spoke at last.

'What's wrong with Faye, Belinda?' He paused, but clearly the question was rhetorical. The car's powerful engine began to tick in the silence as it cooled in the mild evening breeze. Bill had only parked it here a few minutes ago. 'There's something she's not talking about, and I don't understand why. And I *don't* understand why she was so slow to alert us to those symptoms today.'

'No, I was surprised too,' Belinda admitted. 'I wondered this afternoon if something was wrong, then when she belittled her headache I thought I was over-reacting.'

'But was she belittling the symptoms, or was it that she was *more* concerned about something else? You've got no reason to suspect any problem with the baby?'

'No, none! And if Faye had *any* qualms about that, surely she'd. . .'

'Of course she would. You've started doing daily checks of foetal movement?'

'Yes, actually we've been doing two checks a day, because Faye felt happier about that. Half an hour each time, at nine in the morning and nine in the evening, generally.'

'And there's a good healthy number of movements?'

'Oh, yes! The little thing is kicking up a storm!' Belinda told him. 'Faye said the other day that she's going to start a society for the protection of punching bags, because she knows how they feel!'

Tom laughed absently, then continued to muse aloud, 'Dr Greene says the baby is possibly going to be macrosomic, but at this stage that's not a problem and he'll monitor closely in case early delivery is indicated.'

'Faye's prepared for a big baby, in any case,' Belinda said. 'Macrosomic' simply meant unusually large, as many babies of diabetic mothers were. At twenty-four weeks, Dr Greene had begun to make serial measurements of the foetal abdominal and head circumferences, which he would continue at two-week intervals. 'That wouldn't be worrying her now, surely?'

'I don't know. I don't know what it can be.'

'Then don't think about it any more for now,' Belinda advised. 'Some answer might come to you in the middle of the night, and if it doesn't, you can tackle Faye about it tomorrow.'

'You're right. I'm getting nowhere at the moment with this. My mind is going round in circles.' She saw Tom's brow clear and was absurdly gratified to find that her advice was of some use to him. 'In that case,' he went on suddenly, 'to clear my head. . .shall we go and have coffee somewhere?'

'Will anywhere be open this late on Christmas Eve?' she prevaricated, although her heart had leapt instantly at the thought of being with him for a little longer.

'Actually. . .' he glanced at his watch '. . .it's only ten-fifteen.'

'No! It feels much later.'

'I know. . . And I know just the place that *will* be open as well.'

He had assumed her consent to the plan, Belinda realised as he started the engine, and weakly she didn't object. Probably it would be far more sensible to insist on being taken home, instead of torturing herself with his company with his nearness like this, but she couldn't summon the will to argue it out, as she knew he would.

'You look tired and frazzled,' he accused as they drove a winding route through city streets on which the traffic had thinned noticeably now. 'Did you get much to eat earlier?'

'Not much,' she admitted, then added honestly, 'but if I look tired, it's probably the hair and make-up, not me. They weren't designed to last this long, and I changed so quickly into these clothes, just pulled the blouse over my head. . . I must be a sight!' she decided, suddenly horrified. 'Are you sure you want to take me to——?'

'Actually, love, as I more than hinted earlier, I prefer you like this. . .' She had to be imagining the caressing note in his tone. Was he teasing her again?

'You couldn't!' she insisted.

'Well, your hair could use a brush, perhaps, although that mussy halo is rather delightful. But the clothes. . . It's how I'm used to seeing you.'

He glanced sideways at her, and as his eyes lingered for a moment on her form, she realised with horror that she wasn't wearing a bra. The strapless dress hadn't needed one, of course, and in her haste to change, she had dived into this roomy blouse without even thinking of it. Now, her firm, neatly-rounded breasts tingled with awareness and she wanted to fold her arms across her chest to hide their swelling shape.

He swung into a vacant parking space at that moment, right in front of the café that was tucked into an out-of-the-way corner of the city's central business and shopping district. Once inside, Belinda noted with relief that it was lit mainly by the dim, warm yellow of candles in the centre of each table, which would soften the contours of her figure and save her from a self-consciousness that was probably unnecessary in any case. . . Only she couldn't help it, sometimes, with Tom.

He led her to a tiny table in one corner, and she resolutely ignored the fact that nearly everyone else— the place was surprisingly crowded—wore slinky and fashionable black.

'What will you have?' he asked, after they had each studied the menu in silence for a few minutes.

'Black coffee, I think, and something wicked. Cake is always so perfect with coffee at supper time. I'm torn between the Black Forest cake and the hazelnut torte.'

Tom laughed. 'So am I. That's easy, then. One of each, and the wickeder they are, the better.'

And their shared taste for rich cake with coffee late at night restored her faith in their friendship a little, so that when he asked her about her family's plans for Christmas she was able to answer in a relaxed and natural way.

Oh, talking to Tom was so nice! They soon progressed from Christmas to holidays. . .travel. . .world events. . .and then to food, as they laughingly divided the two plump triangles of cake and argued as to which was the nicer.

It was only after he had asked for the bill that he said something that had her on guard again, although there was nothing about his lazy, 'Enjoy the party, did you, by the way?' that should have caused her muscles—including her tongue muscles, it seemed—to instantly tighten.

'Oh, it was very nice,' she assured him.

'Nice? That's a bit bland, isn't it?' he challenged teasingly, his eyes appearing dark and glittering in the dim light of the candles, and his lashes impossibly long and thick.

'Well, perhaps I had a bland time,' she retorted ineptly.

'Bland? In that sexy dress of Faye's?'

She hoped he didn't detect her blush. 'Was it sexy?'

'Greg Carey seemed to think so.' His lazy smile masked unreadable thoughts.

'Oh, him!' Belinda blurted dismissively, disturbed to find that Tom had been aware of at least some of Greg's attentions to her that evening.

'Yes, him! Had you forgotten?'

'Not exactly, but. . .' She took a deep breath. No harm in making it clear what her feelings were about the architect. 'He's not important to me, so I'm not thinking about it any more.'

'Not important?' he echoed again, lightly goading and now lazily lecturing. 'My dear girl, he's one of the best architects in Brisbane, and he hasn't reached the top yet. If you attached yourself to his particluar rising star, you could shoot for the moon.'

'Are you suggesting I should go out with him?' But he only shrugged, so she went on spiritedly, 'Because if you are, then *don't*! I don't like him at all, and if he was going to be the next Frank Lloyd Wright, I couldn't care less, and it wouldn't change my opinion of him as a man, which is that he's——'

'Stop! Stop!' Tom put up a shielding hand. 'I know what he is. An extremely conceited, very lecherous, nearly alcoholic bore, his excellent work nowithstanding.' He paused, then added quite gently, 'But I'm glad to know you discovered all that for yourself without my having to tell you.'

'Why would you have told me in any case? Why would you have made it your concern?' she asked steadily.

There was quite a silence following this, then he said at last, 'Ah, that's exactly what I've been asking myself lately. But unfortunately I haven't quite come up with an answer to the question yet.' Then, changing the mood so abruptly and deliberately that there was no way she could continue to probe him on the issue, even if she had wanted to, he rose and thrust his chair back impatiently. 'Let's go, shall we? The waitress is getting impatient.'

Almost scampering after him, Belinda saw that there was only one other couple left in the café now. She and Tom must have been here for quite a long time, then. She took a covert glance at his watch and discovered that, amazingly, it was nearly midnight. Outside, the tropical summer air was still warm, and they each wound down the car window beside them as soon as they were seated in Tom's low vehicle. He started the engine at once and pulled impatiently out from the kerb, as if still trying to shake off that introspective question of his.

Then, just as the silence between them threatened to become too intense yet again, he said on a soft, teasing, questioning note, 'Frank Lloyd Wright, eh? Arguably the greatest American architect of the twentieth century, but not a name I've heard you drop into casual conversation before.'

She laughed. 'I said it like a final-year architecture student, didn't I?'

'You did,' he agreed.

'Bill lent me some of his architecture books,' she explained.

'A little light bedtime reading?'

'Light bedtime looking-at-the-pictures,' she returned.

'Not making a serious study of it, then?'

'No, but the pictures are interesting, and it's amazing how much you learn from those one-line captions underneath them!'

Tom laughed, breaking the final thread of tension between them, and inwardly Belinda sighed with relief. He definitely wouldn't kiss her now that they were back on this joking footing again. Joking wasn't at all romantic. She had badly wanted him to kiss her, of course—so badly that she knew it simply *must not* happen. . . Not when she loved him, and when he had kissed someone else already tonight, and when all he felt for her was. . .whatever he *did* feel. He didn't seem to know what it was himself, but *she* knew that it couldn't be love, and if it wasn't love then none of the other possibilities mattered.

CHAPTER NINE

But he did kiss her—on the veranda outside her room as she fumbled for the door-handle.

'Leave the door,' Tom growled, then pulled Belinda commandingly into his arms and held her in a close embrace that betrayed every detail of his muscles as they pressed along the length of her softer form.

There was nothing tentative about the touch of his lips, either. They grazed and possessed her mouth as if he was utterly certain of her response to him, and his certainty was fell founded. She surrendered herself to the melting awareness that was building within her, and her exploration of his mouth matched his in eagerness and abandonment.

Soon nothing in the world existed but the heat of their bodies and the fiery threads that seemed to connect her skin to her innermost core. The sketchily covered breasts that had embarrassed her earlier in the evening were now taut and tingling, and when Tom's hands came up to cup them through the thin fabric of her blouse she wanted to arch her back and drink in the new sensation with cries of pleasure.

But finally he drew away from her lips and buried his face in her neck and hair, breathing heavily as if exhausted and spent. 'This has got to stop, Lindie,' he said, using a caressing shortening of her name that he had never used before, and that sounded instantly right on his lips.

'Do we have to?' she breathed, not caring what she was offering to him tonight.

144

A groan was his reply and he began kissing her again, this time letting his lips travel down her throat towards the open neck of her blouse and leaving a hot trail of sensation in his wake. Then he pulled his head up again with a grunt of effort as if it was almost too heavy for him to lift.

'Yes, it does have to stop,' he hissed between clenched teeth. 'You don't know what you're suggesting, Belinda.'

'Yes, I do. I——'

'No, you *don't*!'

'So you understand me better than I understand myself. Is that it?' she demanded.

'No,' he sighed thickly, 'I'm not claiming to understand you. I'm too busy trying to work out why I don't understand myself. That's the problem.'

'And kissing me doesn't help?'

'No, it doesn't!' He wrenched himself from her arms, leaving her suddenly chilled although the night was still very mild, and paced away from her on the veranda, then circled back to stare down at her once again, his face set in a grim, frowning mask. 'How did Bill know where to find me tonight?'

'I. . .I told him.' She was too confused by this sudden attacking question to see at once where it was leading.

'And how did *you* know?' The menacing purr of the question told her he already knew the answer to it.

'Oh,' now she understood, 'because I—was walking in the garden to clear my head and I happened to see——'

'I thought you might have,' he growled. 'I caught a glimpse of your dress as you crept away, but I wasn't sure until just now that it was you.'

'Why didn't you say before that you——?'

But he ignored her. 'I kissed Marise tonight. That

should make you keep your distance, not want to kiss me yourself.'

'Should it? I suppose so. I suppose I wanted to——'

'You're out of your depth, Belinda,' he interrupted harshly. 'Don't you realise that? Get back into shallow water, and *I'll* tell you when it's safe to come swimming.' Then her blank, troubled face drew a rasping laugh from him. 'I'm not making any sense, am I?'

'I'm sorry——' she began.

'It's not *your* fault, love,' he sighed, 'believe me. Now just go into your room, would you? There's a good girl. Forget tonight. I knew I shouldn't have taken you for that coffee.'

'Well, I enjoyed it, so thank you anyway,' she responded stoutly, clinging to the door-handle for emotional as well as physical support.

'Did you? Good girl!' He flicked a finger lightly under her chin, then he was gone, his footsteps heavy on the wooden veranda.

Sapped of all energy, Belinda fell listlessly through the door, let it drift shut behind her and slumped on the bed, utterly confused about what had just happened. One minute he was kissing her as if he never wanted it to stop, and the next he was trying to protect her in some cryptic, jaded way from a danger that seemed clear to him but was a mystery to her.

Or was it such a mystery? She remembered what Faye had said tonight about him being a man of high principles, and gradually it started to make sense.

He's attracted to me, but he knows he doesn't love me. . . If I were experienced and sophisticated like Marise, he might get involved with me anyway, because he'd know that I understood the game and wouldn't get hurt. But he's not prepared to. . .take advantage of me because he knows that I'm inexperienced and that it would be too important to me.

The thoughts came with a fumbling sort of logic and finally fell neatly into place. Fifteen minutes later Belinda fell equally neatly into bed in her lilac cotton and lace nightgown. She didn't fall asleep, however, for a very long time.

'Merry Christmas, Faye!'

'Belinda! I didn't think you'd manage to come today! And a present as well!' Faye began to struggle to sit up, but Belinda forestalled her, relieved that the other woman hadn't commented on the tired bags beneath her eyes that even make-up couldn't fully conceal.

'You're supposed to be resting on your side,' she said sternly. 'Here, if you can't open the present lying down, I'll do it.'

'Would you, love? Thanks!' Faye lay back again and closed her eyes for a moment, opening them as she heard the rustle of paper. 'Here, let me pull the paper off now that you've undone the ribbon and tape, or it won't feel as if it's really for me.'

She pulled at the wrapping, then smiled as she saw the heavy book within. Full of glossy prints and delicate black and white photographs, it was on the subject of German women artists of the early twentieth century, and Belinda knew Faye had wanted it.

'But it must have cost you more than you could afford,' Faye accused.

'Of course it didn't. Bill gave me that bonus cheque last week, and——'

'The bonus cheque was to go to your savings for overseas.'

'Oh, there's plenty of time for that. I haven't made any plans yet. . .'

'No, I've noticed that, and I think I know why. Because you're in love with Tom?'

The sudden question threw her off balance, literally, and she had to sit back hastily in the chair at Faye's bedside to regain her physical and mental equilibrium. Faye was right. The planned trip had never assumed any level of reality of detail in Belinda's mind because, consciously or unconsciously, Tom had been filling her thoughts.

'Yes, I am,' she admitted to her patient in a low, emotion-filled tone. 'Isn't it stupid?'

'Stupid? Why?' Faye demanded. 'Because he's not in love with you?'

The blunt words made Belinda tighten all over, and she nodded, thinking of last night.

Faye went on, 'You're quite sure he *doesn't* love you?'

'Quite.' Pointless to cloud the issue with a description of that scene on the veranda, their kiss and Tom's cryptic words afterwards.

'Hmm. Well, he should!' was Faye's decision. Sweet of her, and it brought a reluctant smile to Belinda's lips. 'See?' the artist said. 'You're smiling! Let's get to work on this right now!'

'Get to work?'

'Yes. Although I have to confess I've already been working on it. I'm sure you know what the problem is between yourself and Tom.'

'Problem?' Belinda echoed again.

'The reason why he's too shortsighted to *see* you there right under his very nose.'

'Oh, he sees me,' Belinda told her with some spirit. 'But he thinks of me as a child, someone too unsophisticated and inexperienced for him.'

'Exactly! Which is why we needed a new hairstyle for you and a new image.'

'You mean when you suggested going to your salon, it was because you hoped. . .'

'Yes, I'm naughty, aren't I?' Faye smiled archly. 'I've been working on this for a couple of weeks now. The next step is that I'm going to start calling you Linda. Belinda's too girlish and Linda's far more womanly.'

'Is it? Yes. . .' Belinda remembered how last night Tom had called her Lindie, making the word a caress. Linda sounded similar, though not *exactly* the same in tone. 'Linda. . .' she echoed.

'May I?' asked Faye.

'If you like.'

'If I think it will help? I do!'

Feeling a little dizzy at being caught in the whirlwind of Faye's enthusiasm, and wondering if she was just imagining a slightly brittle, overwrought quality to it this morning, Belinda listened to several more of Faye's ideas for 'Getting Tom to notice you as a woman'.

I'm sure what she's saying is all hopeless, she decided to herself. But if it helps her pass the time without thinking of the baby. . .

So she agreed to 'Linda', and to wearing more dark colours in future, and to giving her opinion more decidedly about art. . .which led the subject back to the book Belinda had just given Faye.

'Well, I'll treasure this, love,' the artist promised. 'Did you write in the front of it?'

'Yes. Nothing inspirational, just "With love from Belinda" and the date.'

But Faye had already turned to the thick, creamy frontispiece to check for herself before leafing through the rest of the volume.

Belinda watched her, smiling at first because Faye really did seem pleased about the present, then with increasing anxiety. There was something odd in the way Faye was looking. . .no, *peering*. . .at those pictures, shifting the book or her head as if she had to see past some obstruction to get a good look.

And suddenly it clicked. Faye's moments of preoccupation over the last two days, the way she had belittled her headache last night, and her obvious struggles to overcome her concern by talking about other things. . . 'Faye, you've got some vision blurring, haven't you?' she accused gently.

Faye nodded and suddenly began to cry quietly.

'You haven't said anything,' Belinda persisted.

'What's the point?' sobbed Faye. 'What can be done? The blood leakage will dissipate eventually and the blurring will go away, but then there'll be another leak, and another, and every time it happens it brings me closer to going blind one day.'

'What's this?' Neither of them had heard the door open, but suddenly Tom was there, and it was clear that he had heard Faye's last words. 'What is this *ridiculous* talk of going blind?'

'She's had a blood leakage into the vitreous humour,' Belinda explained unnecessarily, her heart thudding at the sight of him. Those eyes looked so blue when he was angry like this, and in a way, after last night, it made things easier that he had come now, when there was Faye's latest problem to think of. 'Both eyes, Faye?'

'Yes. The right one seems worse.'

'When did it start?' Tom demanded.

'The day before yesterday. I woke up and opened my eyes and there were fuzzy patches, just like I had eight years ago. . .'

'Why on earth didn't you tell me?' he demanded harshly, going over to the bed and staring at Faye almost menacingly, his strong back curved tautly over her.

'I. . .I don't know. Belinda asked the same thing. It was stupid—but it just seemed like the last straw, Tom, and what can be done? Gail will probably suggest laser surgery to block off the leaking vessels——' Gail Evans was Faye's ophthalmologist.

'Yes, and to thin out the retina and increase the underlying blood flow. There's no reason to think of blindness, Faye. It's the pregnancy that's responsible for this episode, no doubt. You won't be pregnant for too much longer, and anyway surgical techniques in preventing blindness due to proliferative retinophathy are advancing all the time.'

'But I couldn't have surgery till after the baby is born could I?'

'In your situation I doubt that Dr Greene would advise it, no,' Tom agreed.

'So what's the point in discussing it?'

'Because when you bottle things up, Sis, you get very tense and unhappy, and that doesn't help you or the baby or anyone else!'

'I know. . .' Faye turned her face miserably into the pillow for a moment. 'I was going to tell you about it tomorrow. I didn't want to spoil Christmas, or the party. Belinda's new look. . .'

'We're not children, Faye,' Tom said gently. He looked tired, Belinda noticed. 'We can take one or two clouds on our Christmas cheer. . . Speaking of which, where's Bill? I want to wish him season's greetings.'

'Out on some mysterious errand,' said Faye. 'Back soon, he promised, but that was half an hour ago.'

'Well, I won't stay, in that case. I've seen my patients

and now I've got to drive like hell to get down to Tweed Heads before Jill and Martin conclude that I'm not coming.'

Tom and Faye's parents were living in London for a year, and most of Bill's family lived in Cairns, so there was to be no Russell or Hamilton family Christmas this year. Tom had been invited to share the celebration of old friends who lived just across the state border. Did he really have to leave so soon, though? His eyes had avoided Belinda's face this morning, as if last night was still very much on his mind and he was embarrassed about everything that had happened, and everything that had been said.

Now, he picked up Faye's chart and quickly took in the plotted lines on a graph that were her blood-pressure and blood glucose measurements. He nodded briefly, satisfied with both, then replaced the chart.

'I'll call Gail Evans for you tomorrow,' he said. 'She'll want to take a look at those eyes of yours, whether anything can be done about them at the moment or not, and even if it is Boxing Day.'

But Faye only nodded, and when Tom let himself out gently without saying anything further, the two women remained silent as well. Belinda spoke first, after a pause. 'I'd better do your foot-care routine now, Faye, because I should be going soon too.'

There was a reduced staff on the ward for Christmas, so Belinda had offered to clean and massage Faye's feet as she was now accustomed to doing at home. It didn't take long, and she was just finishing when Bill arrived, bearing a large picnic hamper.

'Is this my present?' While it wasn't exactly a cheer-ful tone, it was more animated than Faye had been since she first admitted that she was having trouble with her eyes, and Belinda knew that she would tell her husband about the problem as soon as they were alone. She would probably feel a lot better for having done so too.

'No, it's brunch,' Bill was saying.

'Brunch? That doesn't sound as if it's on my schedule.'

'It is for today. I've arranged it all with Tom and the staff. Everything fits into your regime, and we'll have it in two stages so it fits with your insulin levels as well. We'll have your presents in between, and I think you'll like them.'

'Oh, Bill!' Faye buried her face in her husband's shoulder, and he whispered some effusive, private words to her.

'I must go,' murmured Belinda, and she wasn't very surprised when neither of them seemed particularly interested in her announcement.

'Hurray! She's here—*at last*!' The twins, David and Michael, had been prowling about in the front garden waiting for the sight of Belinda's car, and as soon as she stepped out into the driveway and came up the path to the house they raced ahead of her inside to relay the news of her arrival, without even saying hello to her.

Belinda smiled. The boys were growing up so fast, but they were still young enough to be intensely impatient at any delay in the opening of the presents, and Dad must have worked hard this morning to persuade them to wait. She plunged happily into the familiar noise and chaos of a house with three boys and unpacked the four plastic shopping bags that contained the gifts she had brought.

'Hello, love,' said her father, coming in from the kitchen where he had been shelling the succulent fresh prawns that would form part of a cold seafood and salad lunch, before the hot turkey dinner this evening.

'Hello, Dad. Merry Christmas!'

Jean Jelbart stood smiling just behind him, her golden-brown hair freshly curled and set for Christmas, and Belinda greeted her warmly as well. They were getting to be quite good friends now, after an initial slightly guilty mistrust on Belinda's part. Just who was this attractive fifty-year-old woman with the warm brown eyes who had found a place in Dad's heart so quickly?

Now those negative feelings had gone, and when she thought she detected an added happiness in their faces today she wasn't afraid or reluctant to guess about it aloud.

'Do you two have some news for me?' she asked with a mischievous smile.

'Hang on! Wait for the champagne!' her father protested, his face giving everything away now.

Just at that moment there was a loud pop, a triumphant, 'Got it!' and an urgent, 'Help! It's fizzing everywhere!' as eighteen-year-old Andrew appeared from the laundry and raced desperately for the six tall flutes arranged on the counter-top in the kitchen. The delicate glasses were filled successfully, however, and Ian Jones announced the news that Belinda had been expecting.

'Jean and I have decided to get married.'

'Congratulations, both of you,' Belinda said sincerely, then Andrew proposed a rambling, outrageous toast and drank a long gulp of champagne with pretended sophistication.

Jean, Ian and Belinda all sipped theirs decorously, while the twins took disdainful tastes and pronounced the stuff vastly overrated.

'*Now* can we open the presents, you lot?' they said in unison, and the rest of the day was devoted to Christmas, with all its trappings of hot turkey in the evening, carols and crackers and funny paper hats, the Queen's Christmas message, and a vast array of dishes to dry and put away.

Belinda stayed the night in her old room, its girlishness both a haven and a restriction. She had outgrown the collection of grey china kittens now, and the pink lace doilies on her dressing-table, and decided that next time she came out here she would clear out the room. Jean would probably like a sewing-room-cum-spareroom, and might want to redecorate it completely. Belinda suspected that the urge to redecorate was something that came to every woman when she married.

On Boxing Day, she returned to the Hamiltons', to learn from Mrs Porter that Bill was at the hospital, and that Dr Greene planned to discharge Faye that afternoon.

'Did Dr Russell ring you at your family's?' the housekeeper wanted to know.

'No, he didn't.' Belinda's heart thudded at the sound of his name, and it seemed like much longer than a day since she had last seen him. And could it only be two days since she had realised fully that she loved him?

'He must have just missed you, then,' Mrs Porter concluded.

'Does Faye. . .or Dr Greene. . .want me to go in to the hospital?'

'No, love.' The housekeeper paused to take a spluttering espresso coffee-pot off the stove, then continued, 'That's why Dr Russell was calling. Dr Greene would only permit Faye to be at home if she kept to a stricter schedule of bed-rest. Dr Russell suggested getting a hospital bed with an automatic reclining section, and it's being delivered this morning. He wants you to help set up the room.'

As if on cue, they heard footsteps on the back stairs at that moment, and Tom himself entered the kitchen after crossing the back porch and knocking briefly at the door.

'The bed's on its way,' he said. 'But the van has to drop off a couple of wheelchairs and things to other places first. . . Hello, Belinda. Your father told me you were already on your way here. . . And you're about to have a new stepmother.'

'You must have had quite a talk!' smiled Belinda.

'Oh, your brother told me that. His name's Andrew?'

'That's right. All the boys are very pleased about it, which makes me happy. . .and I'm pleased myself, of course.'

'Big changes. . .' The words were insignificant, but there was something in his tone that made her happy for some reason.

'Life's like that,' she answered him, and he too seemed to feel that the simple words said more than they usually did.

'Time for some coffee?' Mrs Porter put in. Had she sensed that anything was going on beneath the conventional exchange?

'It's tempting. . .' Tom said.

'*Please* do!' the housekeeper begged. 'Because there's Christmas cake and mince pies to go with it, and with all the kerfuffle over Mrs Hamilton there's been no one to eat them!'

'Can we, Tom? I *love* mince pies!' begged Belinda, seeing that Mrs Porter was feeling unappreciated. She had spent Christmas with her sister's family and her own two children in Toowoomba, but was back on deck today as if the festive season didn't exist, and this waiting for Faye's baby was taking its toll on her as well as on everyone else.

'Of course we can,' Tom agreed. 'Eleven-thirty is probably very optimistic timing for the delivery of the bed.'

The three of them took their coffee and the impossibly generous plate of cake and mince pies out to the enclosed section of veranda beyond the kitchen where Belinda and Mrs Porter sometimes sat during their rare free moments. It was cooled by air-conditioning today, as the temperature threatened to go well above the century mark on the old Fahrenheit scale.

The interlude, stretching in the end to half an hour, was very pleasant. Tom seemed very casual now, as if he had recently found the answer to some burdensome question and could relax at last, and he teased both Belinda and Mrs Porter mercilessly about the Christmas presents they had given and received.

Belinda dared to meet his wicked, twinkling blue gaze, and found that their eyes locked together surprisingly often. It suggested that they shared some sort of secret, but of course they didn't, and when he rose and drained the last mouthful of his second cup of coffee before placing the delicate china cup back in its saucer she could only follow his lead, feeling certain that the relaxed mood was broken.

'We've got to dismantle Faye and Bill's bed, so it can be moved,' he said. 'Bill will sleep in the spare room until the baby's born, and the bed will be stored away.'

'I'll help,' offered Mrs Porter.

'Actually, could you knock us up some cold ham and salad for lunch?' Tom suggested. 'Faye and Bill will be eating at the hospital, but I imagine Belinda will want lunch once the room is ready. She needs a little more beef on her bones!'

'No, I don't!' protested Belinda.

'Well, you certainly don't need to diet!' Mrs Porter came in, eyeing the slim young woman in the cream and sky-blue sundress that set off her sun-blonde hair and fair colouring. 'Of course I'll get lunch, if you can manage everything else yourselves.

'We can,' Tom insisted, and they did.

It was nice to be alone with him in Faye and Bill's room, even though they were only doing the most mundane of jobs—stripping bed linen, dismantling head- and base-boards, and struggling with the big double mattress.

'Oops! Can you manage? Watch your knuckles on the door-frame,' warned Tom, as they half slid, half carried the big mattress safely out of the door, then out on to the veranda and down the back stairs to where it would be stored safely off the ground in a large store-room next to the laundry.

'I'm fine, but watch your head on the——' Too late. The laundry doorway was slightly lower than the doorways upstairs, and Tom had cracked his head sharply on the lintel.

He let the mattress sag to one side and clutched his scalp, swaying dizzily for a moment. Immediately, Belinda was beside him, reaching up tenderly with one hand while trying to support him with the other.

'I'm all right, love,' he said, his teeth gritted against the pain.

'Are you sure? It was quite a crack!'

Without caring what he thought, she threaded her fingers tenderly through the thick, short waves of hair at the back of his head, probing gently with her fingertips for the already swelling lump. Finding it, and telling him bluntly, 'That's going to be the size of an egg soon!' she pulled her hand away again and found touches of blood. 'Oh, no!' she gasped.

'It just broke the skin,' he said. 'Nothing to worry about.'

Then he took a clean white handkerchief from the back pocket of his close-fitting blue jeans, turned to the laundry trough to wet it, and wiped the blood from her fingers. He threw the handkerchief carelessly into a laundry basket, then before she knew what was happening, he was kissing the tips of her fingers, then her palms, then drawing her hands towards him so that she had little choice but to slide her arms around him and receive his kiss.

He had his eyes closed, and for the first few moments Belinda kept hers open, so she could see in extreme close-up the blurred crescents of his dark lashes resting on the smoothly tanned skin of his cheeks. He must still be a little dizzy, she decided. Otherwise, why would his face have that quality of complete relaxation and contentment, appearing almost trancelike?

Then she no longer knew or cared how he looked or what he might be feeling, and surrendered herself totally to the sensation of being in his arms. It felt so safe and so right, and at the same time so electric, stirring her in ways that were becoming increasingly familiar, and increasingly delightful.

'We haven't got time to be doing this,' he groaned against her ear, his breath a whispering caress. 'That bed will be here any minute, and the room needs to be vacuumed.'

'Perhaps Mrs Porter will do that,' Belinda murmured against his lips, letting her fingers trail up and down the sinewed shape of his back.

'Lindie, stop it!' he gasped.

'What? Why?' She pulled back in consternation. 'Did I hurt you?'

He laughed and leaned back against the side of the doorway where they were still standing, with the forgotten mattress sagging beside them. 'Hurt me? You? I don't think you could *ever* hurt me, love!' Then he touched her cheek with a soft palm and added in a low, throaty whisper, 'You might destroy me utterly, I think, but you could never hurt me.'

'That's all right, then,' she answered weakly, not daring to ask what he meant by this last cryptic announcement.

'Open that door for me, could you?' he growled, turning away from her and seizing the mattress in both arms.

She darted past him and opened the door that led to the store-room, then helped somewhat ineffectually as he dragged the mattress through and hefted it on to a stack of boxes.

'This'll do for now,' he said. 'Bill can decide where he wants it later on. Let's go—I think I can hear a van in the driveway.'

He was right. Two workers casually dressed in navy blue shorts and singlets were already in the process of unloading the unwieldy hospital bed. Belinda wondered how on earth they were going to get it up the stairs and through the house, but she sensibly decided that it was their concern, not hers, and anyway the bedroom needed to be vacuumed first. But when she got there, she found that Mrs Porter had just finished the task. 'You seemed to have some trouble with that mattress downstairs,' the housekeeper remarked. 'You were quite a time.'

Belinda turned away to hide her flushed cheeks. 'Oh,

yes. Tom bumped his head.' It was hard to keep the caress out of her voice as she said his name. 'He's going to have a bit of a lump there.'

'Was that it? I almost came down to see if anything was wrong.'

'Oh, no, it wasn't too dramatic.'

Did the housekeeper suspect something? The happy glow left by Tom's kiss ebbed a little, leaving Belinda unsure once more. What had that clandestine moment meant? Was it something sordid and cheap, or something wonderful? Not for the first time she cursed the lack of experience wth men that left her with no clue as to how to interpret what happened between them.

No clue, that was, other than what her heart told her, and as Tom entered the room once more, his eyes coming straight to meet her own, her spirits lifted again and she felt a mysterious sense of rightness about it all.

'They've got it up the stairs and through the front door,' he told them, the practical words giving nothing away about his mood. But Mrs Porter's back was turned as she unplugged and packed up the vacuum cleaner, and the very private smile Tom telegraphed across the room to Belinda told her more than the most sweetly worded compliment could have done.

'Let's hope that vase on the stand in the hall is safe,' she remarked, and he nodded in expressive agreement.

But the bed was manoeuvred into the room without incident, the two men departed after various forms had been signed, and Belinda and Tom began to set up the room. Tom brought in a wheeled trolley on which would be kept all medical equipment and Faye's daily self-monitoring charts as well as new medical charts recording blood-pressure and other observations.

'We'll keep this tucked away in a corner when it's

not needed,' he said. 'No need to remind her that this room is virtually a hospital ward now.'

Belinda found some clean sheets of a three-quarter-bed size that stretched comfortably over the extra width of the hospital bed. They had a pretty pattern of wildflowers on a white background dotted with beige, and there was a lightweight bedspread to match.

'Much nicer than plain white hospital sheets,' she decreed, and Tom nodded.

'You might like to pick some flowers too. That's one thing Mrs Porter always forgets, wrapped up in her marvellous cooking. Faye used to do it, of course, when she was mobile.'

'You mean we haven't had flowers in the house for four months and you never suggested before that I do it?' Belinda exclaimed.

He made a guilty grimace of assent. 'Didn't think of it. Just like a man, I suppose.'

'Or just like a doctor,' she retorted. 'Thinking that healing is all about charts and medicines. I never mentioned it because I thought perhaps Faye didn't like flowers in the house. She uses them in her paintings, I know, but I'd wondered if generally she was allergic, or something. . .'

'No, nothing like that.'

'I'll make sure there are flowers around from now on, in that case,' Belinda said firmly. 'Because *I* love them! I'll go and pick some right now.'

'I feel thoroughly put in my place,' sighed Tom.

'And so you should!'

He laughed, and Belinda took some scissors from a kitchen drawer and ran lightly down the back stairs to find her flowers. She was familiar enough with the garden by this time to return in only a few minutes with sheafs of colourful tropical blooms, and she

arranged them in two big vases to make riotously
informal bunches of colour that lacked classical form
but would, she hoped, be pleasing to Faye's artistic
eye.

Her heart felt amazingly light, and she knew it was
because of Tom and the way they were talking and
laughing together over the morning's task. He stayed
for lunch, and then at about two o'clock Bill and Faye
arrived, the latter walking from the car to the house
but going straight to the bedroom to lie down. She
didn't protest about the new, more strictly controlled
bed-rest, and went about her preparations in a quiet,
businesslike way.

'I'd better do a blood glucose straight away,' she said
as soon as she was lying in bed, with the adjustable
part tilted to a gentle angle.

Belinda wheeled the trolley over and helped Faye by
passing her the lancet and reading the reagent strip for
her. The glucose level was normal for the time of day,
and everyone was pleased.

'And what did Dr Evans have to say this morning?'
Tom wanted to know.

'Well, they wheeled me over to Ophthalmology so
she could have a good look,' Faye told him. 'And she
thinks the leaking vessels are in the same places as
before, which I suppose is good news. At least it's not
spreading.'

'Sounds good to me. . .'

'But I'm so glad to be home,' Faye confessed on a
long sigh. 'Hospital reminds me far too strongly of my
days before self-monitoring.'

Belinda nodded, knowing by this time that Faye had
been hospitalised several times for keto-acidosis and
other diabetes-related problems brought on largely by
her former wildly fluctuating blood-sugar levels.

'You've done the room beautifully, love,' Faye went on.

'Tom did just as much as I did,' Belinda assured her.

'And got myself a bump on the back of the head for my pains.'

'What? Did Linda hit you?' Faye exclaimed, using her new 'sophisticated' name for her nurse with slightly arch emphasis.

'Linda hit me? What on earth are you talking about, Faye? I bumped my head on the door moving your mattress through the laundry,' said Tom.

'Oh, yes, that doorway is rather low.'

'But what's this "Linda" business?' The impatient tone was familiar, and brother and sister were clearly back on their normal footing of fond, energetic squabbling now that the latest crisis in Faye's pregnancy had settled down.

'Oh, don't make an issue of it, Tom!' Faye groaned exaggeratedly to him.

'I'm not. I'm simply asking why you've suddenly started calling her Linda.'

'Not suddenly,' Faye protested untruthfully. 'I've been doing it for some time, haven't I, love?'

'Some—er—time, yes,' Belinda nodded, feeling foolish. Actually, she was beginning to decide that she didn't like being called Linda at all.

'Well, it's ridiculous!' snorted Tom.

'Oh.'

Faye's disappointment brought a covert smile to Belinda's lips. She wanted to tell her that perhaps the plan—the dark colours, the new name—wasn't necessary any more, that there was an awareness between herself and Tom today that almost made her believe he *did* share her feelings, but with Tom himself in the room, and Bill as well, and Mrs Porter coming in now with Faye's mid-afternoon snack and a pot of tea for everyone, there was clearly no opportunity.

In any case, she wasn't *sure* yet, and she rather thought she'd like to experience more of those private looks and smiles, and hear more of those conventional remarks of his that concealed the caress in his tone.

So she sat down very happily with her tea when she saw that Tom had accepted a cup as well and had brought in an extra chair from the sitting-room.

'Now you must tell me about your presents,' Faye decreed, turning to Belinda.

'Tom will be bored,' she protested, tasting his name sweetly on her tongue. 'He's already heard about most of them. . . Oh,' she added, 'except that somehow I never mentioned what I got from Dad. The most beautiful set of travel bags—a suitcase, an enormous duffel bag, and a smaller shoulder bag with what claims to a snatch-proof inner passport pocket.'

'Oh, for your overseas trip,' said Faye. 'Lovely!'

'When are you going?' Bill wanted to know.

'Oh, I haven't made any definite plans yet,' Belinda answered.

'Don't put it off too long and let the chance slip by,' Faye's husband advised. 'It's the ideal time for you. You're young, with no real responsibilities here. Your family wouldn't hold you back, and you have a professional qualification that's highly in demand wherever you go, if you wanted to stay a few years and work. England, America. . .that sort of freedom of travelling, with only your own whim to consult, tends to dissipate as you get older. I went when I was twenty-four. . . My God, it's twenty years ago now! I hitch-hiked round Europe, lived off the smell of an oily rag, as they say.'

'Mmm, it sounds great!' Belinda nodded, with the

best performance of enthusiasm that she could muster. She thought that seeing Europe and England would be nice, of course, but the vagabond style of travel, the freedom of being on one's own, and being away from her family and homeland for years, didn't appeal at all. It sounded frighteningly lonely and rootless to her, although she saw why Bill, as an adventurous and newly qualified architect, would have found it so stimulating.

Her enthusiasm must have been convincing, however, as Bill threw back his head and laughed. 'Good girl! Send us a postcard—several postcards! Venice and Vienna and Paris. . .'

'Oh, Bill, stop reliving your lost youth!' Faye put in crossly, and Belinda repeated meekly,

'I really haven't made any definite plans.'

Then Tom spoke. 'Well, you should make them, Belinda. Bill's right—it's an opportunity that won't come again. There's nothing here that should stand in your way.' He left the room abruptly before anyone could respond, and it was only when Belinda heard his powerful car start up in the driveway that she realised he wasn't coming back. She didn't see him again for four days.

CHAPTER TEN

'WHY don't you hurry and put on that new outfit before Tom comes?' Faye suggested to Belinda.

It was after five-thirty on a Friday night, and Tom was expected at any minute. Mostly he just turned up casually, but yesterday Faye had suggested that he make plans to stay for dinner. 'Mrs Porter's itching to do something special,' the artist had explained. 'I think she misses our normal social life more than we do.'

So Tom had agreed, but Belinda felt unhappy about the whole thing. She knew that Faye had issued the invitation to Tom as a deliberate part of her campaign to bring the two of them together, and somehow she had to summon the courage today. . .or soon. . .to tell her patient that it just wasn't working, it was pointless, and she would prefer it if Faye gave up the idea. In fact, she should have said all this to Faye weeks ago.

It was already February, and Faye had had no problems since her return from hospital on Boxing Day. Dr Greene came with increasing frequency to the house to examine his patient, and although the baby was large for its gestational age it seemed healthy and active, with a strong, regular heartbeat. Dr Evans had made several visits as well, and was able to report that the damage to Faye's eyes did not seem to be worsening. The blood leakage that was clouding her vision had drained away now, and everyone was holding their breath that there would be no more episodes of the problem.

The days for Belinda and Faye were surprisingly full.

Now, for example, they had just finished a sponge bath in bed, there was a pre-dinner blood glucose test to do, as well as the pre-dinner insulin injection—right arm, site four, this evening—and the foot-care routine still to fit in. Faye could not paint or draw while lying in bed, but in the mornings Belinda usually read to her for an hour while she rested her eyes, then left her alone for the remainder of the morning to rest or scribble ideas for future painting projects.

After lunch, Faye had her nap, which had stretched to two hours now, as she was sleeping poorly at night, and after she woke she usually liked to have Belinda in to chat over the mid-afternoon snack. It was at those times, or times like the present as they went about the health-care tasks that were now so routine, that she most often brought up the question of this campaign over Tom.

'You are happy about the outfit, aren't you?' she demanded anxiously now.

Last Saturday, she had sent Belinda to one of her favourite clothing boutiques, with the instruction that she was to let Hélène guide her in her choice. The result was a pair of lace-edged, calf-length black tights, very stretchy and very shiny, topped with a dramatic beaded blouse—the fabric was black silk and the beading multi-coloured and dangling—as well as the highest heels Belinda had ever worn.

The ensemble gave her a slinky, model-like elegance and made her feel like an actress playing a part. . .a nightclub scene, probably. . .instead of her normal self. She had decided, in fact, to return the outfit, and Faye's mentioning it like this forced the issue so that finally she found the courage to speak.

'Well, it's very gorgeous,' she said. 'And if I saw it on, say, Julia Roberts or Demi Moore in a film I'd think it was wonderful, but it's not *me*. And in any case,' she rushed on, 'it's hopeless. You must have seen, noticed by now, how cool Tom is with me. I couldn't even say we were friends now. He hardly ever stays to talk the way he used to. You've wangled him into dinner tonight, but of his own accord he would have gone straight off. . .to. . .to Marise, probably.'

'Marise? Rubbish!' snorted Faye.

'They're having an affair, or they were. . .'

'They were not! She threw herself into his arms at every opportunity, and like a gentleman he kissed her back. I dare say he even enjoyed it! She's very lovely and I'm sure she kisses like a veteran, but if you mean he's been sleeping with her, no! That's not Tom's style. He'd have to care for her a lot more than he does to do that.'

'That's nice to know—I suppose,' Belinda responded slowly to Faye's energetic outburst. 'But it doesn't make any difference to Tom and me. You must have noticed that it's not working, Faye.'

There was a small silence in which the artist conceded defeat, then she spoke. 'Love, I'm sorry. My brother's a fool, if it's any consolation. I suppose the best thing for you to do is to book a plane ticket to London for around the beginning of April and forget about him that way.'

'I already have,' said Belinda. 'I booked one last Saturday after I went to Hélène's boutique.'

'Is it my fault, do you think?' Faye asked anxiously. 'Did he rebel because he guessed I was throwing you at him?'

'Don't be silly! I don't think Tom's the kind of person to act on an impulse of contrariness like that,' Belinda soothed sincerely. 'It just. . .wasn't meant to

happen, that's all. So do you mind if we don't say
anything more about it?'

'Of course not. I've probably lacerated your feelings
enough on the subject already. And take the outfit
back. Wear that pretty peacock blue dress of yours
tonight. That brings out the colour of your eyes so
beautifully, and it's casual enough to look as if you
haven't dressed up. Put on some make-up too, and that
silver and lapis lazuli necklace your father gave you.'

'Perhaps I shouldn't dress up at all,' Belinda
responded, glancing down at her pink linen trousers
and cream blouse.

'Come now, girl!' Faye scolded. 'You must at least
be elegant in defeat!'

And they both managed a laugh.

Tom arrived half an hour later, when Belinda was
still changing. She heard his car in the drive and
recognised the sound instantly. It was a more commanding note than that of Bill's Mercedes. Tempted to
hide in her room and avoid meeting him until the meal
was served, she knew she must not.

Although he seemed to avoid personal conversation
with her now, one thing he always wanted to discuss
with her was Faye's day, with a rundown on his sister's
mood and any abnormality at all in her blood sugar,
blood-pressure or anything else. Fortunately, today the
rundown could be short, as Faye's condition had given
no cause for concern at all.

Belinda met him in the front hall on his way to his
sister's room, and as expected he raised questioning
eyebrows. 'No problems today?'

'No, none at all. She almost lost count of the baby's
movements this morning when she monitored them.
Really, it was one continuous wriggle. Blood sugar's
been fine. I'm massaging and grooming her feet twice

a day now because lying in bed is creating some roughness on her heels and the sides of her feet that could get inflamed and sore if we're not careful.'

'Good—I'm glad you're alert about that. Should we have her podiatrist in for a look?'

'Not at this stage. I've been doing all the routine things a podiatrist would do.'

'Perhaps I'll take a look at her feet myself, then, just in case,' Tom decided.

'Of course.' She said it courteously, using the same polite professional tone that he was using himself, all the time hating the fact that he never teased her now. It was always like this these days—two colleagues who respected each other but didn't really have much to say. 'Come and see her now,' she went on. 'I'm going to go and. . .and see if Mrs Porter needs any help in the kitchen.'

Mrs Porter didn't. She never did, being as efficient as she was creative in the kitchen that she loved so much. A cold gazpacho soup accompanied by hot, crusty garlic bread and followed by several special salads was on the menu for tonight, and Belinda arrived in the kitchen just as Mrs Porter was garnishing with parsley a deliciously chunky bowl of boneless chicken, artichokes, avocados, celery and cashew nuts coated in a tangy dressing and resting on a bed of purplish mignonette lettuce. There was Caesar salad, lobster salad, and carrot and raisin salad as well, and Belinda thought that if only Tom weren't here, her mouth would be watering hungrily. As it was, the presence of the tall endocrine specialist had robbed her of most of her appetite.

Still, she made a creditable attempt at the meal, which she ate with Bill and Tom buffet-style, grouped around Faye's bed. The latter was lively and talkative tonight, and Belinda suspected that it was an attempt to lighten her own spirits after their discussion about Tom. Tom himself was barely responsive to Faye's mood, and when the artist scolded her brother about it, he only growled, 'I'm tired. I usually am at the end of the week, and this one has been particularly tough. I should have resisted your blandishments last night and opted for a quiet Friday evening at home.'

'Oh, you're *impossible* Tom!' Faye pushed the wheeled dinner tray aside and flung herself over in the bed to face away from her brother. 'What you need is——'

She stopped abruptly, and Belinda thought it was because she had been about to say something outspoken that would betray this afternoon's confidences—'A wife like Belinda,' or 'Someone to share your house and your life,' but when Faye did speak again her tone was not the breezy cover-up that Belinda had expected.

'Hang on,' she said cautiously. 'Help! Could this be. . .? I think my waters have broken.'

She sounded half alarmed, half excited, and within seconds Tom was beside the bed pulling back the sheets. But the liquid spreading rapidly on the pretty floral sheets wasn't the sweetish, colourless amniotic fluid. It was blood, bright red, in frightening quantities.

'Belinda, call an ambulance!' Tom commanded, but she was already on her way out of the room.

This was a third-trimester bleed from the placenta that was still positioned dangerously low in the womb, partially blocking the cervix, and Belinda knew it was potentially serious. At the very least, intravenous fluids would be needed, and, from the look of that blood, probably a transfusion as well, although tranfusion was always a reluctant option these days.

The bleeding might then stop spontaneously, but this time there would be no question of coming home, even for the most disciplined bed-rest. It was almost laughable that so much could go wrong for poor Faye, and it was becoming a miracle that the baby was still so strong and vigorous.

When she returned to announce, 'The ambulance is on its way. It'll be here in minutes,' Belinda saw that Faye had begun crying quietly, and that Bill was pressing her hand wordlessly between his two trembling ones. Tom brushed past Belinda in the doorway, his frowning mask of a face barely acknowledging her presence.

'I want to talk to Greene,' he said, 'and to the blood bank.'

The minutes crawled like tired snails, but the ambulance arrived before Tom had returned from making his phone calls in the study, and with the compassionate yet businesslike speed that Belinda never ceased to admire, the paramedic ambulance officers slid Faye on to a stretcher and carried her to the waiting vehicle, where an intravenous line could be set up immediately. Bill accompanied his wife, and as the red lights of the ambulance faded down the street, Tom emerged from the study at last.

He looked grim, and Belinda demanded, 'What's wrong? What does Dr Greene say?'

'I haven't spoken to him yet. He's out tonight and hasn't responded to his pager yet. The hospital will give him my car-phone number and he'll call me as we drive in. . . I hope.'

'Do you want me to come?' she asked.

'I presumed *you'd* want to.'

'Yes, of course I do. I hoped I wouldn't be in the way.'

'No, Faye finds you very reassuring. Actually, she may not be able to see much of you, but *I* find you reassuring too.'

Her heart thudded, but she ignored it. 'And the hospital knows a blood transfusion will probably be needed?'

'Yes, but that's the other problem. No blood. Even type O. . .' which Belinda knew was the universal donor group '. . .is low at the moment. A heart has just become available for transplant, with a patient waiting for it, so they want to hold blood for that, and for the weekend, when they're more likely to need it for trauma cases. Then there was an emergency two hours ago. Road trauma—a family. And three of them needed A-Negative, Faye's blood group. The nearest supply of that now will have to be flown in from Rockhampton.'

'A-Negative is my blood group. . .' Belinda began.

'You're joking!'

'*Would* I? *Now*?'

He gave her a speaking glance and they both rushed for his car, neither needing to discuss the question of whether Belinda was willing to donate her blood for Faye. For several minutes they drove in silence, then Tom began to speak his thoughts aloud, glancing briefly at Belinda every now and then but mostly keeping his narrowed eyes firmly fixed on the road. It was sunset, and an orange and gold landscape of cloud and sky flamed in the west, but they were barely aware of it.

'I really don't like this,' he said. 'It's more than the last straw for Faye. How did she look as they took her downstairs?'

'Very pale. Not speaking. Not crying any more either. Listless.'

'I think that baby should be delivered tonight! If only

Greene would phone back so we can discuss it! He likes to bring diabetic patients as close to full term as possible. He prides himself on delivering on the optimum date to balance the welfare of mother and baby, and his percentage of vaginal deliveries over Caesarean is amazingly high—which is great, these days. But I'm not sure that Faye can take much more waiting.'

'Physically?' Belinda queried.

'Emotionally. Physically. Both.'

'She was thirty-four weeks on Tuesday.'

'And she's pretty sure her dates are accurate. But with the size that the baby is already, it's likely Greene would have a hard time getting her beyond thirty-eight weeks. Effectively we're talking about bringing this on three and a half weeks early. The baby'll be big enough, but its lung maturity is the real question. Hyaline membrane disease is something we don't want.'

'He may decide to hold off for a few days and give steroids to develop the lungs,' Belinda suggested.

'Yes, that's distinctly possible,' Tom agreed.

'Is a vaginal delivery out of the question for Faye?'

'At the moment, I imagine so, yes. If we wait, the placenta might still shift enough, though that's unlikely at this stage. Surely Greene will have to see it my way!'

As if on cue, the car-phone gave a discreet purr to punctuate Tom's passionate sentence, and he snatched it up as he braked at traffic-lights which had just turned red. 'Damn!' The juggle with phone and gearstick was impossible, and adroitly Belinda took the receiver while he controlled the car.

'Dr Greene?' she said politely. 'Dr Russell needs to speak to you urgently about his sister, Mrs Hamilton.'

'Put him on, then, would you?' the exalted obstetrician said impatiently.

'Here he is. . .' He was ready now, and had his hand held out for the instrument, lightly brushing her fingers accidentally as she passed it to him. Her hand tingled at once, and she pressed it angrily into her thigh, trying to forget his meaningless touch.

'Greene?' said Tom. 'Yes, she's on her way to the hospital. Almost certainly a placental bleed. . .' He paused to listen for a moment. 'I should think so, and we have a donor. . . But listen! I think we need to seriously consider the possibility of delivering the baby tonight.'

Belinda listened on tenterhooks to one side of the discussion as Tom somehow managed to present his case forcefully while driving at the same time. Professionally, her opinion carried little weight, but she had to side with Tom on the issue out of her concern for Faye, and her familiarity with the artist's problems. Surely Faye had already been through enough!

'Yes, I realise it's principally an obstetric issue at this stage,' Tom was saying, 'but from the point of view of her diabetes the advantages are all on the side of delivering now. There was the proliferative retinopathy episode a few weeks ago, and when she was hospitalised for the threatened toxaemia we found that her blood glucose was actually better controlled at home now than in hospital. . . Exactly. Home care is really out of the question now, and another period in hospital is *not* good for this patient's emotional well-being!' He listened again. 'Of course—you have to examine her first. But I want to give you my professional opinion——' He broke off testily, then added, 'Sure, yes. It's personal as well. . . OK, then. See you in a few minutes.'

He slammed the phone back into its cradle, and Belinda winced.

'Greene's on his way,' the endocrine specialist reported. 'He won't make a decision until he's seen her, though he's having the surgical team paged and prepped. Fair enough not to decide on the phone on the basis of my say-so, but——' He didn't finish.

'It's going to be all right, Tom,' Belinda said gently. 'Don't forget to have faith in Faye. None of what's been happening to her lately has sat well with her temperament. For *years*, in fact. She's the kind of person who'd probably forget to eat or sleep for days while she was painting, then eat ravenously for the next week to make up, if she could. But she can't because she's diabetic, and she's adapted to that with huge success. She paints, and she's incredibly good at it.'

'You know that, do you?' he queried.

'I ought to! I've spent enough time watching her paint *me*!'

'Hmm. . .'

'And she's adapted to spending seven months virtually imprisoned in bed, or at least on the couch. . . If Dr Greene tells her it's best to wait another four weeks for the sake of the baby, she'll grit her teeth and wait another four weeks,' Belinda added.

'I know.'

'You're not afraid of. . .something tragic, are you?'

'Of course I am,' he said in a low, passionate voice. 'Faye's been inches from death twice before with this disease, I've seen other patients die—not many these days, thank God—and even if it was "*only*" the baby she lost. . .'

He swung into the hospital driveway, and Belinda couldn't find a comforting utterance in response to the deep fears he had just tried to voice. She ached with sympathy for him, and if this had been Christmas, or any time in those months when she had felt they were friends, she would have pulled him into her arms and soothed him with soft hands and whispered words. Tonight, though, that seemed out of the question, and as they hurried into the hospital through its large, brightly lit main foyer, they walked several yards apart.

Faye had been taken to Labour and Delivery, where she waited in a private room for Dr Greene's arrival. She continued to receive fluids intravenously, and a sample of her amniotic fluid had been taken and was being tested to determine the baby's lung maturity.

When Tom and Belinda reached the lift, he took her arm suddenly and said, 'Belinda, can you go across to the blood bank now and give that blood? It'll take a while to be ready for use with everything they do to it these days, and if she does need it, the sooner it can be ready, the better. If she doesn't need it. . .'

'I'll have given it for someone else who needs it just as badly,' Belinda finished for him.

Accordingly he disappeared into the upward-travelling lift, while she waited for one to take her down a floor where a corridor linked this building to the next one, in which the twenty-four-hour blood bank was located.

Ten minutes later she was relaxed on a bed with a cannula attached painlessly to her right arm, taped in place near the soft inner crook of her elbow. Every few seconds or so she squeezed a hard rubber shape that the blood bank nurse had given her, an action which would pump the blood faster into the cannula, through plastic tubing and into the attached plastic bag, which was slowly filling.

Nurse though she was, and even though she had been giving blood fairly regularly for several years now, Belinda never liked to watch the bag fill, so she managed to hold a magazine in her left hand. In fact, though, the print was a blur before her eyes, and her thoughts were with Faye. . .and with Tom. He must be talking to Dr Greene by now.

An older nurse came to Belinda to see how she was progressing. 'A few more minutes to go,' she said, her face cheerful beneath dark hair scraped back into a rather severe French roll. 'How are you feeling? Not faint at all?'

'I'm fine,' Belinda assured her.

'Dr Russell phoned down a minute ago,' the nurse said. 'He asked if you can give an extra two hundred and fifty millilitres.'

'Did he say anything else?'

'No—I think he was pretty rushed. Do you need to talk to him?'

'No, don't worry. I'm happy to give the extra,' said Belinda.

'Though we'll need to keep an eye on you for a good while afterwards and replenish your fluids thoroughly. Why don't you have a juice now?'

'Lovely! Thanks.'

'Now I've got to go,' said the nurse. 'We've put out a call to the hospital personnel that we're low on blood and some of them have volunteered to come in. Things might get busy here soon.'

'Don't worry about me. If there's any problem, I'll call you.'

'I'll check you again in five minutes or so, then.'

The nurse left to assist another donor and Belinda sucked from her juice box through its thin straw. If Tom had asked her to give extra blood, then they were definitely planning to transfuse, but this told her nothing about whether the baby would be delivered that night. Would Tom phone again to tell her what was going on?

She wanted to jump straight up from this padded
and sheet-covered bench, once her blood donation was
completed, and go up to Labour and Delivery to see,
or at least hear about, Faye, but she knew from
experience that giving blood left her drained and tired,
and giving two hundred and fifty mils extra tonight
would really sap her physical rsources. Determined to
recover as quickly as possible, she sucked harder on
the juice and asked the nurse for another one as soon
as she was finished.

'Another hundred mils to go,' said Sister Farrer.
'You're slowing down a bit now. Pump your hand on
that squeeze block.'

Belinda nodded, closed her eyes and held the juice
in one hand and the squeeze block in the other. Her
thoughts drifted to Faye. Was she lying like this
receiving intravenous fluids and simply waiting till the
haemorrhaging stopped?

'Lindie?' It sounded husky and emotion-filled.

Belinda's eyes flew open at the sound of the familiar
voice. She hadn't heard Tom's approach. . .and he
hadn't called her Lindie since Boxing Day.

'Hi!' she said.

'How are you?'

'I'm fine.'

'Make sure they give you extra iron tablets,' he told
her.

'That's not important. How's Faye?'

He took a deep breath. 'Dr Greene has decided my
way. She's being prepped for an emergency Caesarean
now, under epidural. Lung maturity looked good, but
the placenta was still bleeding heavily. Faye's morale
was very low. . .'

'Poor Faye!' sighed Belinda.

'. . .until Dr Greene told her he'd decided to deliver,

then she perked up immediately and insisted on an epidural so that Bill could be there and she could see the baby straight away.'

'That's wonderful!' Belinda laughed, blinking back the sudden tears that had started to her eyes, and hoping that Tom had not seen them.

'So. . .' He turned to the plastic bag that now bulged with deep red fluid and read the increments marked on the side. 'Looks as if you're done.'

'Is she?' Sister Farrer hurried over. 'Good. Let me deal with it, Doctor.'

She began to disconnect the cannula rather fussily and put a band-aid on Belinda's slightly bruised arm as Tom stepped back. Belinda wanted to tell him not to worry about waiting for her if he wanted to return to Labour and Delivery, but somehow the words wouldn't come.

'Sit up slowly, dear,' Sister Farrer was saying, and Belinda obeyed.

The movement made her feel a little light-headed, and she remembered too late that she hadn't had much appetite for those hearty, delicious salads that Mrs Porter had made earlier. Still, there was always food here at the blood bank as well as plenty of sweetened fluids to quickly restore energy. She hopped down to the floor, but it seemed further away than she had expected and now suddenly it was rising up crazily to meet her. Or was it melting away altogether. . .?

'Belinda! Belinda! More juice, please, Sister Farrer!' The voice, at first urgent, then tersely commanding, sounded close to her ear, and she was cushioned in something warm and soft and firm and strong. Tom's voice. Tom's arms.

'Oh, no! Did I faint?' she asked weakly.

'For a moment, love.' The voice was tender now. 'I shouldn't have asked you for the extra two-fifty mils.'

'I'm fine, really,' she protested.

'You will be, once I pump you full of every calorie this place has to offer, and your first iron tablet straight away.'

'How silly of me!' She said it to cover her tremulous awareness of the fact that she was still in his arms, and began gently to try and pull herself away, but he seemed strangely reluctant to let her go. He must think she was going to faint again. More firmly she pressed her hands against those hard, tanned forearms and took a step forward, then the ceiling lights danced and the room was suddenly misty again.

'It seems as if I really do need to lie down,' she said faintly, and then he had swept her off the ground and was carrying her to one of the low, comfortable sofas in a private alcove where donors who were feeling faint could eat and drink in peace and quiet as they recovered. He deposited her on the sofa, then pulled a low coffee table over.

'Put your feet up on that,' he ordered. 'I'll ask Sister Farrer if there are some pillows.'

'No, I'm——'

But he didn't even wait to hear her protests that she was all right, and came back a minute later with two hospital pillows which he arranged for her, and she thought the faintly male, musky and intensely sensual smell of him as he bent over her was making her more faint than loss of blood.

Next he brought her sweetened, milky and deliciously hot tea as well as two sausage rolls, two ham and mustard sandwiches, and three chocolate-coated doughnuts.

'I'll never eat all this!' she protested feebly. 'Specially the doughnuts.'

'Yes, you will, Lindie,' he ordered tenderly, then added on a lighter note, 'There's one thing about junk food—it gives you a quick fix of carbohydrates and sugar. Eat something more nourishing for supper, though.'

'Supper? You mean I'm to eat *more*?'

'And even more importantly, drink! I'll get you more tea in a minute.'

'Don't you want to get back to Labour and Delivery?' she asked.

He shook his head. 'Faye's epidural should be nearly in place by now. This is her experience, and Bill's, and it's the surgical team's job to get the baby delivered safely. Anyway, I'd rather stay here with you.'

There was a caress in his tone that she hadn't heard since Boxing Day, and then he sat down beside her and pulled her across so that she was cradled against him instead of against the cool white pillows. With her heart thudding so loudly that she felt sure he must feel it through her ribcage, she took another gulp of tea and waited, knowing he must speak, explain somehow what it was that had suddenly flared between them again.

But when he did speak at last, his words were a chilling disappointment. 'Have you finished making your plans for going overseas yet?' The bland tone gave nothing away. How could he be making small talk when their bodies were pressed together like this?

'Yes,' she forced herself to reply brightly. 'I booked my ticket last Saturday. I leave on April the eighth, flying to London.' The great city's name echoed in her ears, sounding like the bleakest place in the world.

'One-way ticket?'

'No, it's an open return, but it's quite generous. It has to be used by——'

'Do you have to go on the damned trip?' Tom burst out suddenly. 'Do you want it so badly? How can you chat about it like this when I'm holding you and when I want to kiss you and make love to you so badly I can't even think of anything else!'

'You were the one who asked me about it,' she returned, as angry and impatient as he was. 'And no, I don't want to go! I've *never* wanted to go. Not by myself, as Bill talked about, like a homeless nomad.'

'Then why on earth have you booked a ticket?'

'Because I thought I *should* go,' she retorted. 'And because once I realised. . .I was in love with you, and when I was sure you didn't love me back, there seemed no point in staying.'

'And what makes you think I don't love you back, Lindie?' he whispered softly, twisting her gently in his arms so that his lips were very close to her own. 'Because I *do* love you, you know. I've loved you since August, and I've *known* I loved you—and what I wanted to do about it—since the day after Christmas.'

'What *do* you want to do about it?' she asked in a small voice, not yet quite daring to believe what she was hearing.

'Marry you, of course! You will, won't you, my darling? *Say* you will!'

'I will, Tom.' But she was barely able to finish the short, beloved syllable of his name. The word was drowned against his lips and her response to his kiss was utterly happy and complete.

'I shouldn't be doing this to you,' he growled at last.

'No one is looking,' she whispered.

'No, but you might faint again.'

'Well, if I do, I've chosen a pretty safe place to do it

in, I think,' she responded tenderly, exploring the commanding contours of his face with fingers that had been aching to do this for months.

'Oh, very safe,' he agreed. 'The safest place in the world. . .and the world is where we'll go for our honeymoon, because I'm determined to get that travel bug out of you so you'll stay safe and happy with me for the rest of our lives!'

'Tom, for the last time, I don't *have* a travel bug!' Belinda protested.

'But right from the beginning, the reason you wanted the private nursing job. . .'

'If you want the whole story. . .' Briefly, she told him about Deana Davenport.

'But why did it matter that she teased you, love?' Tom wanted to know.

'Because I *did* have a crush on you! The most enormous one!'

'Don't you still? I hope you do. . .'

'No, I don't,' 'she said seriously. 'Now it's love, and that's very different.'

'I know—it is. Faye must have told you about my marriage. . .'

'Yes, she did.'

'I was an idiot, and I was lucky to get off so lightly. If we'd had children. . .'

'You made a mistake,' said Belinda. 'But fortunately for me, Sylvia made a far bigger one when she left you.'

'The irony is that I didn't realise till Christmas, when I knew I loved you, that it was someone like you I should have been looking for all these years since.'

'Why did you realise at Christmas?' she asked, nuzzling her mouth into his warm neck, and thinking it tasted far better than the doughnut she had been dutifully consuming.

'It was Faye, dear, silly Faye, with her ridiculous attempt to doll you up into the sort of woman she thought I'd want. "Linda!" I struggled with the whole thing the night before Christmas and the whole of Christmas Day, and finally I realised then that I wanted you just as you were. I was going to tell you so that day Faye came home from hospital—Boxing Day. I was *sure* you felt the same way. I hoped so, and I was going to take the risk of finding out, but then Bill started talking about your once-in-a-lifetime chance to travel, and I thought about the fact that I'm thirty-four and you're twenty-two. . .'

'I like a mature, *older* man,' she teased.

'Don't make me feel I've got one foot in the grave already! And it seemed that I'd be standing in the way of your freedom and your opportunities. I decided it was unfair of me to say anything, and that if you wanted the trip so badly you probably *didn't* want me. Then tonight, after nearly two months of holding back, trying to forget, trying to pretend, when I saw you lying there so pale. . . You're still pale, love.'

'I'm fine now,' she assured him.

'And then you fainted. And I didn't care any more. I had to say it, and I decided to be selfish. I was going to *make* you prefer me to London and Paris. . .and I was going to get a fellowship overseas if I had to, to keep you.'

'Let's just have a European holiday instead.'

He laughed and kissed her again, and somehow it was another hour before the last of the doughnuts and her third cup of tea were consumed and he decreed that the colour had returned to her cheeks and they could leave. 'Do you want to see Faye?' he asked.

'How can you even ask?'

Labour and Delivery was quiet tonight, and so was Recovery, to which they were directed by the matronly grandmother of five who presided over the ward. After washing their hands and putting on hospital gowns and caps, they were able to go in, and found Faye and Bill alone together in the dimly-lit room.

No, they were not alone. . .'

'Isn't she beautiful?' Faye whispered, her eyes misting and her throat going froggy as she showed them the tiny black-haired bundle cradled tightly in her arms.

'Her name's Catherine, and she weighed seven and a half pounds,' Bill put in, intensely proud.

'It was so quick!' Faye went on. 'They put the anaesthetic in. That took about half an hour, and I couldn't feel a thing from the waist down. They had drapes up, so I couldn't see anything gory, and Bill was there, and suddenly there was a wail. . .'

'And she was born!'

'Bill was with the paediatrician while he examined her,' Faye went on.

'And she's perfect, though she'll be in Neo-natal Intensive Care for twenty-four hours, they said,' Bill frowned.

'Yes, that's routine for diabetic mothers,' Tom assured them. 'Nothing to worry about.'

'It took quite a while to stitch me up, but everything's all right now, although they say I've lost a lot of blood from the placental bleed.' The happiness Faye felt at Catherine's safe birth masked her underlying weakness and exhaustion.

'They're going to transfuse?' asked Tom.

'Yes, as soon as it's ready. Belinda, thank you!'

'Oh, Faye, please—don't be silly! Just show me the baby!'

Faye pulled the flannelette blanket aside a little, already tender and protective of her child, and Belinda bent down to take a closer look. The baby was sleeping, its lids tightly closed and its little face red and perfect at the same time. As she watched, Catherine nuzzled and snuffled, and Faye put a finger in the baby's mouth for her to suck. They all watched and smiled, and after a while Tom broke the silence with an impatience which told happy Belinda that he simply couldn't wait to break the other important news of the evening.

'By the way,' he said, 'Belinda isn't going to London any more after all. Giving blood makes her go all woozy, it seems. She's lost her head utterly and decided to marry me instead!'

Unfortunately for his sense of the dramatic, it turned out that neither Faye nor Bill were terribly surprised. 'We guessed,' said Faye, 'when you were more concerned about getting down to the blood bank than about thrashing through my prognosis with Dr Greene.'

Tom laughed, just as a young nurse timidly entered the room. 'We'd better take Catherine away now, Mrs Hamilton,' she said. 'She's really supposed to be in Intensive Care, and we have to check you over soon, as well. You'll see her at one in the morning for her first feed.'

With a last tearful cuddle, Faye parted with Catherine, then sighed back against the pillows. 'It's over, and I'm safe, and she's safe,' she said. 'But I'm not doing this again!'

'No, you're not, Faye,' Tom said seriously. 'I'm glad ʼʷ said it yourself. I'm not sure that your body could ⸜ther pregnancy.'

'I *know* it couldn't!' Faye said frankly. '*I* couldn't. Catherine is going to be a beloved only child.' Then she added slyly, 'But she'll have several cousins to play with, I hope.'

'It's possible,' Tom said cagily, and Belinda laughed.

'Not too much younger than Catherine, either, please,' Faye ordered.

'I'd say a year or two at the most,' Belinda put in.

When Tom whispered, 'As long as that?' in her ear so that only she could hear, she turned her face up to his for his kiss and blessed Deana Davenport and her ill-natured tongue from the bottom of her heart.